3 5674 00607592 4

W9-BXM-699

**DETROIT PUBLIC LIBRARY**

BROWSING LIBRARY
5201 Woodward
Detroit, MI 48202

**DATE DUE**

# THE
# WHISKY
# MURDERS

# THE
# WHISKY
# MURDERS

## RICHARD GRINDAL

Walker and Company
New York

*C.2*
*M*

## For Sheelagh Óg

Copyright © Richard Grindal 1984, 1987

All rights reserved. No part of this book may be reproduced or transmitted in any form or by any means, electronic or mechanical, including photocopying, recording or by any information storage and retrieval system, without permission in writing from the Publisher.

All the characters and events portrayed in this story are fictitious.

First published in the United States of America in 1987 by the Walker Publishing Company, Inc.

**Library of Congress Cataloging-in-Publication Data**

Grayson, Richard.
  The whisky murders.

  I. Title.
PR6057.R55W4   1987          823'.914          86-32568
ISBN 0-8027-5661-1

Printed in the United States of America

10 9 8 7 6 5 4 3 2 1

BL OCT 26 '87

# 1

THE GLASS DOORS separating the living-room from the patio were open and a hard, bright light fell across the swimming pool and the grass beyond, without doing more than touch the dark mass of pine trees. Nor did the loud voices and strident laughter of the two men in the room do more than interrupt the endless rustle of the crickets, for the villa was set high up in the pine wood, well away from the houses on the lower slopes of the hill near the road that led to Cascais.

They were two Scots drinking together; two Scots who had met in a hotel bar in Estoril and started a convivial evening that had grown more convivial the longer it lasted. True the elder man, Fraser, was a Highlander, brought up in the Free Church, while Bryce was a Catholic from Clydebank, but small ethnic and religious differences could be overlooked by exiles in a foreign land. Several whiskies bought mainly by Bryce, an engineer from a ship anchored in the Tagus, as he explained, and therefore with money to spare, were followed by an excellent dinner in one of the fish restaurants around the harbour, with two bottles of Vinho Verde and one of the best Portuguese brandy. Afterwards they had driven in Fraser's Mercedes, cautiously because he was canny enough to realize that he was a little drunk, back to the villa which he had bought when he came to live in Portugal six years previously.

Now they were drinking another bottle of brandy which Bryce had insisted on bringing back from the restaurant, and it was he who poured the measures. Perhaps because they had been talking about Scotland for most of the evening, they had turned now to life in Portugal; of how Fraser had become one of the British colony in Estoril, of how he played three times a week on the golf course, supported the cricket team and subscribed to the British Hospital where his wife had been so well looked after during her terminal

5

illness. A sentimental man, like so many otherwise combative Scots, Fraser, who had been less than generous with his affection to his wife while she lived, grew maudlin as he spoke of her death and wept.

'I brought her out to this paradise,' he complained tearfully, 'to live among the exiled royalty of Europe. At great expense, mind you. And what does she do? She dies on me in less than two years. She leaves me alone.'

It took longer to get the man fou than Bryce had expected. Then at last, when the brandy bottle was almost empty, Fraser announced that he would fetch another from his kitchen, rose to his feet, took two paces forward unsteadily and fell face down on the carpet. Bryce shook him roughly without getting more than a moan in response, but as a precaution he waited a full five minutes until the drunken stupor was as effective as unconsciousness.

Lifting the limp body and carrying it into the bathroom required no feat of strength, for the old man was slight in build. He had chosen the bathroom because it had a window on the side of the villa nearest to the garage and the added bonus of a gas-fired water heater. Leaving the house, he went to the garage where, he had learnt from a reconnaissance carried out the previous day, there was a length of garden hose pipe. The late Mrs Fraser had spent much of her time trying in vain to make a British garden in the red, stony soil. Bryce had brought with him, and concealed under the passenger seat of the Mercedes, a simple contrivance, specially made to connect the car's twin exhausts to one end of the hose. Once this had been fitted, it was a simple matter to drop the other end of the hose through the bathroom window, switch on the car's engine and let it run. Then he sat down on the porch of the villa to wait.

When it was over and he had satisfied himself that Fraser was dead, he systematically and carefully removed all traces of his visit, rinsing his brandy glass and putting it away, sliding the doors to the patio shut, drawing the curtains and switching off the lights in the living-room. In the bathroom he first took off Fraser's jacket, tie and shoes and carried them into the bedroom to give the impression that the dead man had gone into the bathroom to draw himself a bath and then he turned on the water heater. Finally, after wiping everything he had touched during the evening, he left the house, coiled up the hose,

6

replaced it in the garage and walked down to the main road through the pine trees, avoiding the dusty track which led past the other villas.

The hired car was still where he had left it earlier that day, concealed in another clump of trees a mile or so away. In a few minutes he was driving along the road to Lisbon where he would cross the bridge over the Tagus and head for Spain. He drove carefully and at a moderate speed, knowing that an accident was the only possible unforeseen factor that could upset his plan. In any event there was no reason for haste. Fraser's body would not be discovered until the Portuguese maid arrived at the villa in the morning. After that it would be at least an hour before a doctor or an ambulance made an appearance and another hour, more probably two, before the police went to the villa, even supposing they were called. And if anyone should be suspicious about the cause of Fraser's death, well, Bryce knew that the Department of Legal Medicine in Lisbon already had a backlog of more than 4,000 cases.

He might stop to allow himself the luxury of a couple of hours' sleep before morning. In any case he would certainly have time for a leisurely meal at Madrid airport before he boarded the plane for London. If the Glasgow shuttle was behaving itself he might be home in time for a few pints in the pub with his friends.

The bar in the Mansion on Turtle Creek was full, as it was most evenings around six-thirty. Well-heeled young businessmen who had dropped in for a drink on their way home from the office mingled with others who had already collected their dates or their wives and were on their way to dine, either in the hotel itself or at one of the many excellent restaurants in Dallas.

John Marshall Friend junior was there talking oil with his new associate, Dave Litman, who had just flown in from Houston where he had successfully negotiated an excellent contract for their company. Mostly their negotiations were successful, for they were two of the smartest young operators in the off-shore oil business.

At the table next to theirs a silver-haired Scotsman was sitting with two executives of a New York public relations agency. Marshall Friend and Litman watched as the Scotsman patiently told the elegant and very pretty waitress that he wanted a particular brand of

Scotch whisky and that it should be served without ice but that he would like some water on the side. When the Scotch arrived with a separate tumbler full of iced water, the Scotsman explained courteously to the girl that he wished to add the water to the Scotch himself to make sure he had exactly the right amount and for that purpose he would like a small jug of water with no ice.

'The gentleman wants a pitcher of water,' one of the PR people interpreted for the waitress.

'When I was in Houston,' Litman remarked to Marshall Friend, 'I was given a Scotch in this guy's home that I'd never tasted before. It really was something!'

'Did he tell you the name of the whisky?'

'I guess he did but I've forgotten it.'

'Most likely it was a malt whisky.'

'I didn't know you were into Scotch, John.'

'I learnt a lot about it — the hard way.'

'How was that?'

Marshall Friend explained that when his father had died, he had found among the old man's personal papers correspondence relating to an investment he had made some years previously. The investment had been the purchase of five hogsheads of Scotch malt whisky. Marshall Friend senior, it appeared, had bought the whisky after reading a prospectus issued by Bonnie Braes Whisky Incorporated, a company with an office in New York. The prospectus had claimed that anyone shrewd enough to put money into buying Scotch whisky could make a very substantial profit after twelve years when the whisky was mature.

'So my dad bought the whisky,' Marshall Friend told Litman. 'The deal was that they would keep the stuff for him at the distillery in Scotland and when it was mature he could sell it. This Bonnie Braes outfit even promised in the brochure that they would buy it back at the going price.'

'But it didn't work out that way?'

'I guess my dad forgot all about it. After all, the money he invested was peanuts. But when I found the papers I thought I'd get in touch with these Bonnie Braes people to see what the whisky was worth. It kind of intrigued me.'

'Don't tell me!' Litman grinned cynically. 'Let me guess. Bonnie Braes had gone out of business.'

'Right. They had vanished. I nosed around and found out that there had been a number of companies in the States working the same racket. Then the Securities and Exchange Commission had started to get interested in them and they folded up their tents and slunk off into the night.'

'And it was a rip off?'

'I didn't leave it there. I decided I'd find out if my dad really had been conned.' One could not tell from Marshall Friend's expression whether he would have been disappointed or pleased to find that his father had been fallible enough to fall for a confidence trick.

Soon afterwards, he explained, he had taken the opportunity while on a business trip to Aberdeen to make a detour to Edinburgh where he had consulted a firm of solicitors. A junior partner of the firm, a young man named Strachan, had been most helpful. As Marshall Friend had made an appointment to see him in advance, he had made a number of enquiries about the activites of Bonnie Braes Whisky Inc. and similar firms who were promoting the same kind of investment, and had learnt a great deal.

The sale of new whisky 'fillings', as they were called, was, he had assured Marshall Friend, a perfectly legitimate business, but companies like Bonnie Braes had deceived potential investors when they suggested that there was a role for private capital in the market. All the Scotch whisky blending firms who produced and marketed the different brands of Scotch bought the fillings they required and financed their stocks themselves out of their own resources or by bank borrowings.

'There's no market in whisky futures,' Marshall Friend told Litman, 'as there is for many other commodities. So when these comedians persuaded private speculators to order new whisky, they were just creating a pool of surplus Scotch which the industry would never need.'

'Did you try selling your old man's stock?'

'This guy Strachan had already approached one or two firms of whisky brokers. Oh yes, they were ready to buy the whisky, but they offered a price marginally lower than my dad paid for it.'

9

'Some racket!' Litman could not keep his admiration out of his tone.

'You'd better believe it! You see what the poor saps who fell for it didn't know was that Bonnie Braes were making them pay almost double what the distilleries were charging at that time.'

'Couldn't you have sued Bonnie Braes?'

'No way! Not under Scottish law anyway. An American attorney might have been able to file a suit here if we could have tracked down any of the partners, but it wouldn't be worth it for a few hundred bucks. They were clever, those guys. They pretended that the Scotch they were peddling was hard to get and wouldn't let any one client have more than five casks. Who would sue for that kind of money?'

'So what did you do? Cut your losses and sell for what you could get?'

To sell had been Strachan's professional advice, but he had also made another suggestion. Marshall Friend could have the whisky bottled under bond in Scotland as a single malt and shipped to the States for his private use. Strachan had guessed rightly that the young American was rich enough to indulge himself and vain enough to enjoy the cachet of having a Scotch which he could offer to his friends at home as a rare malt whisky that had been specially distilled, matured and bottled in Scotland for Marshall Friend junior, as the individually designed label would show. Of course the whisky was not of the highest quality, not on a par with the great Highland malts, Macallan, The Glenlivet, Glenfarclas, Glenfiddich, Cardhu, Mortlach, Glenmorangie, Aultmore and Talisker, but neither Marshall Friend nor anyone who might visit his home would be likely to know that. Marshall Friend had liked his suggestion and the deal had been arranged with a whisky firm who specialized in the private label business.

'How much of the stuff do you have?' Litman asked.

'More than a hundred cases. A famous Scottish artist designed a label for me. It shows a Highland scene with a sketch of the distillery itself — Glen Cromach. I'll send you over a case if you like.'

## 2

THE RAIN HAD come without warning, as it so often did in the Western Highlands, a bank of cumulus cloud appearing suddenly above the ridge of mountains and sweeping in to envelop the glen in a sullen, grey overcast from which the rain slashed down in fine, slanting lines as merciless as flails. In the afternoon, 3,000 feet up on Sgurr nan Ceathreamhnan, there had been the exhilaration of achievement and of the wild beauty of Wester Ross, the contours of its peaks and crags etched to an incredible sharpness in the clear air, the lochs silent in blue loneliness. Now as the rain cascaded down on Sanderson's packframe, with his wet breeches clinging to his thighs and bedraggled grass clutching at his boots, hill walking was no more than a dreary, sightless drudge.

He knew that there must be a bothy not much more than a mile away in the glen, for he had marked it on his map when he had planned his route with Maggie and Simon and other friends in Glasgow. That had been no more than a precaution, for he had a lightweight tent with him and for the last nine nights he had slept as he had intended, camped in wooded glens or by a burn and once above a waterfall. Tonight though he would need shelter and a fire to dry his clothes and himself.

The bothy when he found it was better than he had expected. Mountain bothies, he knew from old, were unpredictable, some no better than ruined, foul-smelling hovels in which one was hard put to endure a night even with a blizzard raging outside. The one he found that evening was a cottage, a standard Highland butt'n ben, primitive enough with its earthen floor, but boasting two rooms, one with a fireplace, a table and two benches, the other with wooden bunks and, at one end of the building, a byre now used as a wood store. Not expecting sanitation, he was not disappointed and a burn running through the glen a few yards away would provide water.

After heaving his packframe off on to one of the bunks, he fetched wood from the byre, lit a fire, took off his sodden cagoule, emptied his boots of water and sat down by the fireplace to dry out. This was not how he had planned to spend his last evening before heading south. With ample daylight left, he had intended walking on until he reached a point from where he would have been able to watch the sun sinking behind the jagged ridges of the Cuillin on Skye, one of the most spectacular sunsets which Scotland had to offer. Instead he sat in the smoky room, steam rising from his clothes, shivering and watching as the fire hissed and spluttered, for most of the wood was still wet.

Now that his ten days of hill walking had almost ended, he recalled the reason which had prompted him to start the walk. It had been intended to serve a double purpose, to provide hard and sustained exercise that might help him regain something resembling physical fitness and also ten days of solitude during which, from what he now sensed was a watershed in his life, he could reflect on the mistakes which had embellished it in the past and decide how he would spend what remained of it in the future.

Physically, he knew, he was in immeasurably better shape. Since he had left the train from Inverness at Acnasheen and set out, northwards first in the direction of Loch Maree, he had climbed no less than ten munros, the name given in Scotland to mountains of more than 3,000 feet, a modest achievement in summer some might think, but even so, looking down at his waist and his thighs he could see he had lost weight. At least ten pounds of fat, perhaps twelve, had melted away; blubber accumulated carelessly but insidiously in London, through lunches at the Connaught and the Savoy Grill; dinners at the Boulestin and Le Gavroche; entertaining that was supposed to persuade clients to use or consider using the services of the company for which he worked and which, in general, appeared to succeed in that objective.

Sanderson was less sure that the second purpose of his walk had been achieved. Solitude had not, as he had hoped, been conducive to sharp analytical introspection. Instead the splendour and timelessness of the Highlands had filled him with a tranquillity that he could not remember experiencing before. He had found himself absorbed not in his personal problems, but in the fascinating details of what he saw around him, the changing colours of the distant hills, the different cries and

12

songs of birds which he could not always see, the number and variety of wild flowers, the sound of burns trickling through the heather and the peat.

So the questions about his past and future, which had occupied his mind when he left Glasgow nine days ago, now seemed remote and unimportant. As he sat gazing into the flames of the fire and trying to recapture the concern and sense of urgency he had once felt about the future, he heard someone come through the entrance of the bothy into the bunk room behind him. There was a sound of stamping, a good deal of shaking off of water and some quiet swearing. Presently the newcomer came into the living-room, still carrying his packframe by the shoulder straps in one hand and a wet woollen balaclava in the other. When he saw Sanderson, he seemed disconcerted and stopped in the doorway, as though trying to decide whether he should stay in the bothy or go back out into the rain.

'Good evening,' Sanderson said. 'Foul outside, is it not?'

The man did no more than return the greeting curtly. Then, evidently deciding that he would stay, he went back into the other room, put his packframe down on a bunk from where he could still see Sanderson through the doorway and began unpacking it. He was a man of about fifty, with a typically Scottish face, a complexion that was if anything too red, and short, curly hair that had once been sandy and was now shot with grey. As he was spreading his sleeping-bag on the bunk, he glanced suspiciously at Sanderson from time to time. In Sanderson's experience people whom one met in the Highlands, whether they were natives of that part or had come there to walk or climb or fish, were almost invariably friendly and relaxed. The man who had just come into the bothy had reasons no doubt for the suspicion and resentment he could not conceal and they would probably emerge during the long evening that lay ahead of them.

Presently the man came back from the bunk room. 'Have you been here long?' he asked abruptly.

'About thirty minutes. I was already in the glen when the storm broke.'

'From which direction have you come?'

'The north. I spent three days around Loch Maree.'

The answer appeared to satisfy the man. He took a bench, placed it

13

on the other side of the fire and sat down facing Sanderson.

'My name is Sanderson, by the way. Bruce Sanderson.'

'I'm Iain MacNair.' Suspicion had not abated far enough to allow the offer of a handshake.

A long silence followed. Having cautiously pushed out a slender bridge which, if they wished, they might use to communicate, Sanderson was not prepared to press matters any further. MacNair for his part seemed to have no inclination to share his thoughts.

Eventually he asked another question. 'How many days have you spent up here, then?'

'Ten in all. This is my last night. Tomorrow I head south. And you?'

'I had planned to stay another week, but I may decide to cut it short.'

'If this weather continues, you would be well advised to abandon the Highlands.'

'It's not just the weather.'

MacNair made the remark as though it were directed only at himself, as though he were thinking of some problem or obstacle to his plans which other people would not comprehend even if he were to explain it. He brooded over his thoughts for a time and then suddenly, as though this were the only recourse left to him, pulled a flask from his hip-pocket and began to unscrew the cap.

'Will you take a dram?' he asked Sanderson.

'That would be very welcome. Thanks.'

The cap of the flask had been designed to be used as a cup and after filling it with what looked like whisky, MacNair passed it to Sanderson. His hand shook slightly as he did so and some of the liquid splashed on to the earthen floor. The first sip he took told Sanderson that it was whisky but a whisky stronger and more pungent than any he had tasted before, assaulting both his taste buds and his throat.

MacNair must have noticed his almost imperceptible grimace for he smiled. 'Sorry. I should have warned you that the whisky is well above normal strength, about a hundred and ten proof.'

'It's a malt whisky, is it not?'

'Yes, a single malt.'

Sanderson was no expert on whisky but he knew that a single malt whisky was the unblended product of one of the hundred-odd pot still distilleries in Scotland. 'Which one?' he asked.

'Glen Cromach. You may never have heard of it. It's one of the few small independent distilleries left. What do you think of the whisky?'

'Very good! I like it.' Sanderson did not feel that he was imposing too much on sincerity. The flavour of the whisky was pleasant enough and, as every Scot would be ready to swear, all Scotch whisky was good, although some brands might be better than others.

MacNair appeared delighted by his reply. 'As you lit the fire,' he said, 'I'll make supper for both of us.'

'No, that's too much!'

'Not at all. I insist.'

'Then at least use up what's left of my provisions. To hump everything back to Glasgow would be senseless.'

In the end they pulled out all the supplies they had been carrying in their packframes and examined them. Sanderson had brought mainly powdered and dehydrated foods with him, for a friend who was an experienced hill walker had advised him that a packframe weighing no more than forty pounds would be as much as he could comfortably carry. So he had been existing largely on dehydrated packet foods which, however tasty they might be with their artificial flavourings, never seemed to satisfy his appetite, and had only diverted from his planned route once in the ten days to buy fresh and tinned food at a village shop.

'We'll have a real feast tonight, I promise you,' MacNair said as he made a selection from what their two packs had to offer.

He seemed to enjoy preparing the supper and did it well. After hurrying out into the rain to fetch water from the burn, he lit both of their tiny Butane Gaz stoves and soon, following a cup of packet soup, enriched to some recipe of his own, he served up two generous plates of stew and they finished their meal with a handful of raisins and a bar of chocolate each. Then they sat facing each other by the fire drinking instant coffee laced with another shot of malt whisky. MacNair had pulled back his sleeves when he was preparing the meal and Sanderson noticed that he had a long, jagged scar on his right forearm, running almost the full length from wrist to elbow.

'What line of business are you in?' he asked Sanderson.

'I'm a chemical engineer by training but until a couple of weeks ago I was working in London for a firm of management consultants.'

'And then you gave it up?'

'It would be more accurate to say that the firm gave me up. I was made redundant.'

Sanderson tried to make his reply no more than a statement of fact. Although he knew it was absurd at a time of world recession to believe that redundancy carried a stigma, the painful memory of the day when he had been told by Jack Smart that Macro Consultants had decided to terminate his contract still made it hard for him to talk about it without indignation and a sense of shame. After all, less than a year previously Smart, the managing director of Macro, had told him that the Board rated him as the best of the younger consultants and had hinted that he might be invited to join it before too long.

'I had a not dissimilar experience,' MacNair said sympathetically. 'The company put me in a position from which I had no option but to resign. I suppose one could call it constructive dismissal.'

'What kind of business was that?'

'The whisky business.'

'MacNair's whisky?' Like everyone else in Scotland Sanderson had heard of MacNair's Gold Label Scotch Whisky, one of the leading brands in both the home and export markets.

'Yes. My great-grandfather started the company, but a few years back my father sold out to North British Breweries. It's a familiar story. His father and his uncle, who were both in the business, died within a few months of each other and the death duties were crippling.'

'It's a bit rough to be forced out of a business that once belonged to you. What did the brewers do?'

'They decided to lump MacNair's in with a vodka company which they own in the north of England and some small firms of wine importers that come under their wing. So they set up a company to manage the whole wine and spirit group and appointed an infant prodigy of an accountant as top man. I had been running MacNair's but now the new man took all the decisions that counted and I was his office boy.'

MacNair spoke without bitterness. He appeared to be reconciled to the treatment he had received and could look at it with detachment. Sanderson wondered whether in time he would be equally philosophical about what had been in reality a much less savage blow to

16

his pride. Perhaps it was only in middle age that a man could accept injustice with equanimity.

MacNair may have sensed what he was thinking, for he said, 'Mind you, it cost them, I can tell you. When he sold the business my father negotiated a grand contract for me and the brewery had to pay plenty to break it. No doubt they thought it was worth it at the time but I'm asking myself what they feel now that MacNair's Gold Label's share of the home market has dropped a percentage point or two.'

'What would that mean in terms of sales?'

MacNair shrugged his shoulders. 'Maybe forty thousand cases a year. Perhaps a little more. Mark you, I'm not claiming that happened because I left the company. North British Breweries have suffered right across the board. Their beer sales are down, wine no more than holding its own and they've been forced to close at least ten of their pubs and sell several others.'

'And what are you doing now yourself?' Sanderson asked.

'Still in whisky. I'm one of the directors of the Loch Rannoch Whisky Company.'

'There are no distilleries around Rannoch are there?'

'No, nor whisky companies either.' MacNair laughed. 'I suppose Peter Wandercliff, who started the company, chose the name just for its Scottishness.'

The fire was dying, the burnt logs crumbling with no more than a sigh into glowing embers. MacNair picked up two more from the small pile that Sanderson had stacked by the hearth and threw them on. A flame flickered briefly, throwing shadows into the corners of the room. Outside the rain was still beating down and they could hear the rushing of the wind among the trees in the glen.

'Resigning from MacNair's was a turning point in my life,' MacNair remarked.

Not long ago, Sanderson remembered, he had been thinking of his redundancy in the same terms. 'In what way?' he asked.

'For all my working life I had been a traditionalist, part of the whisky establishment. I assumed when I left MacNair's that I would soon get an offer from one of the other major companies. I didn't. It was only Peter Wandercliff who wanted my knowledge and experience. And he was a man whom we had always regarded as no more than a fringe operator, a small entrepreneur on the edge of the whisky trade.'

'His was a pretty small outfit, was it?'

'Yes. He started as a whisky broker a few years ago and then branched out into the private label business.'

'Private labels? What are they?'

'Many customers, particularly overseas, restaurants, bars, social clubs, like to have a whisky that is exclusive to them. So the supplier provides a blend with whatever name they care to choose, usually the name of their establishment and a specially designed label.'

'What's the attraction? Snob appeal?'

'It used to be. But then the big supermarkets in France and Belgium and Germany caught on to the idea. They of course want to import direct and cut out the agent and their orders can be substantial. In that way they can sell their own whiskies at prices well below those of the standard brands.'

Sanderson knew of friends of his who had bought Scotch at unbelievably low prices on the continent to bring back home. More often than not they had complained that the whisky had turned out to be pretty rough, lacking in flavour and fiery to swallow, but he decided it would be tactless to say so. Instead he asked MacNair, 'Is the business profitable? To the supplier in Scotland, I mean.'

'Certainly, if one can get the volume orders. We've done pretty well out of it. Of course, the big names look down their noses at it.'

MacNair explained that the old-established whisky companies, although they supplied Wandercliff with whisky from the distilleries which they owned, frowned on the private label business. One of their complaints was that supermarkets were exploiting the prestige of Scotch that had been built up over the years by the advertising and promotion of the major brands.

'I used to think that way,' he added, 'but since I began working with Peter my views have changed. I took a long, hard look at the whisky trade's traditional attitudes.'

'And what conclusions did you reach?'

'That we in the business had been blinded by success. We had begun to take it for granted that the world demand for Scotch would continue to grow, that we had nothing to fear from the competition of other drinks.'

'And that isn't so?'

18

'I only wish it were! In the past few years other drinks, spirits like vodka and white rum, have made enormous strides. Their sales have grown faster than those of Scotch. And they have one great advantage over Scotch. They can be produced more cheaply. And do you know why?'

'Because they don't have to be matured, I suppose.'

MacNair looked at Sanderson sharply. 'How did you know that?'

'It was just an educated guess. I know Scotch has to be matured because I've seen the warehouses around the distilleries in the north and they are stacked high with casks of whisky. Keeping money tied up in stocks must be expensive, especially with the cost of money what it is today.'

'Well, you're right.' MacNair had been talking freely, carried away by his enthusiasm and his belief in himself. Now suddenly his earlier suspicion seemed to reassert itself. He said grudgingly, 'But the whisky industry is in for a shock, I can tell you. I've been working on two ideas which will revolutionize the trade.'

'I wish you success.'

'My ideas can't fail. I shall succeed all right if I'm allowed to.' He paused before he added, 'But, you see, they are trying to have me murdered.'

It was a statement of fact, made without emotion or histrionics and, as far as one could tell, not intended to impress or even to arouse curiosity. MacNair sat leaning forward, his elbows on his knees, staring into the fire. Sanderson glanced at him, hesitating to ask a question or even to comment, in case this might be taken by this strange man whose feelings and impulses seemed constantly in conflict, as an attack on his privacy.

He did not need to say anything, for presently MacNair continued, 'If there had been just the one incident I might have concluded it was an accident, but two escapes from violent death within a few days is more than coincidence.'

'When did they occur?'

'The first attempt to kill me was one night when I was driving home from a dinner party. An enormous road transport vehicle, one of those juggernauts, was driven head on into my car.'

'Deliberately?'

'Yes. Without any shadow of doubt. I was driving along a straight stretch of road when I saw this monster coming towards me. When it was not more than a hundred yards away it swung across the road towards me.'

'What did you do?'

'I was frightened out of my life. The road was narrow with only a couple of yards of grass verge on my left separating it from a ditch. On the other side of the ditch was the boundary wall of a country estate. Whoever was driving the juggernaut had picked his spot well. All I could do was to swerve on to the grass verge but even so he hit me. By some miracle I was flung out of my Bentley and right over the wall. If I had not been in an open car and if I had been wearing a seat belt I would have been killed. The Bentley was a write-off but I landed softly in a clump of rhododendrons. The juggernaut didn't stop but drove off into the night.'

'And the second attempt on your life?'

'How well do you know this part of the country?' MacNair asked.

'Hardly at all.'

'Then you will not be knowing the waterfall to the west towards Loch Affric?'

The falls, MacNair told Sanderson, were spectacular, a huge curtain of water plunging from the side of the mountain 200 feet or so into a rock pool below. They could be seen from a distance, but to get the most impressive view one had to scramble down a narrow, treacherous path, suitable only for people with mountaineering experience, to a ledge of rock less than fifteen feet from the column of water, where one could feel the spray in one's face and be deafened by the noise. That morning MacNair had made the descent to the ledge, intending to photograph the falls.

'I was lining up my Leica,' he told Sanderson, 'when I looked behind me. I don't know why, for against the noise from the falls one would not have heard anything. Call it instinct if you like. Anyway, there was a huge boulder, at least three feet across, hurtling down the path towards me.'

'What did you do?'

'The ledge is tiny with a sheer drop of two hundred feet to the rocks below. There seemed to be no way I could avoid being struck by the boulder, nothing I could hold on to. I flattened myself against the side of the hill, waiting to be crushed or knocked off the ledge. And then the boulder must have hit a spur of rock jutting out from the main wall, for it was deflected, not very far but enough. It still landed on the ledge, brushing against me as it passed and then bounced, leaping into space. If I had not seen it coming it would have taken me with it.'

For the first time that evening MacNair appeared to be affected by emotion. His voice was still controlled, his sentences slow and measured, but one could see fear in his eyes and his temples were moist with perspiration. Sanderson decided he would give the man time so that the vivid memories of his two escapes from death would recede and neither of them spoke for several minutes.

Then Sanderson asked, 'Have you any idea who the person who is trying to harm you might be?' To speak of killing or murder would be melodramatic and privately he still had not decided how much of the story he had been told was the exaggeration of a frightened or neurotic man.

'Oh yes, I know who it is. And it's not just one person. But I could never prove it.'

'Then what will you do? How can you protect yourself?'

'Let's not discuss it,' MacNair said suddenly and decisively.

'Of course. If you would rather not.'

'We've talked enough about me. Let's talk about you.'

They talked about Sanderson, of how he had been born in the Western Highlands, educated at school in Fort William and at Aberdeen University, of how he had worked for four years in Switzerland with a pharmaceutical company before joining Macro Consultants. Sanderson told MacNair of the consulting assignments he had carried out, several of them with major British companies looking for higher productivity or increased efficiency or a better management structure, and of his uncertainty about what he wanted from life in the future. MacNair was, surprisingly, a good listener; surprisingly, for Sanderson had begun to think of him as self-centred, introspective and perhaps slightly panaroid, the kind of man who would be too obsessed with his own problems to have sympathy for those of other people.

Not long before midnight MacNair made them both another mug of coffee; instant coffee again with powdered milk and artificial sweetener but welcome, for the warmth and smoke in the ill-ventilated room had dried both tongue and throat. The rain had dwindled to a fine drizzle but Sanderson decided that even if it were to stop, he would not go and pitch his tent outside. In the bothy he was at least spared the attentions of the swarms of midges which had feasted on his neck and arms every evening since he had arrived in the Highlands.

As they were drinking the coffee MacNair asked, 'Where could I get in touch with you back in civilization?'

'You could ring me at my friend's flat in Glasgow,' Sanderson replied and gave him Maggie's number.

MacNair gave no reason for his request. Soon afterwards they turned in and, weary from the cumulative effects of ten days of exertion, Sanderson fell instantly asleep. He woke once during the night and seemed to hear somebody moving in the other room of the bothy. The fire was dead but enough moonlight had filtered into the bunk-room for him to see that MacNair was not in his bunk. The noise from the other room sounded like a vigorous scraping, not unlike a dog scratching with its front paws in the ground. He thought of rousing himself and going to investigate but laziness and torpor engulfed him and he drifted back to sleep.

His last thought was, 'The silly old sod is burying the rubbish; in the hut and at this time of night!'

He awoke soon after six to a beautiful, still dawn with only the birds and the tumble of the burn in the glen to disturb the silence. MacNair had already left the bothy, but not before he had cleaned out the fire. Nor was there any rubbish to be seen left over from the remnants of their meal. MacNair had worked thoroughly, even sweeping the floor of the room where they had sat by the fire, as though he were determined that nothing would be left, no trace, no footmarks to show that he had passed that way.

# 3

IN PRINCES STREET gardens beneath the shadow of Edinburgh Castle an Aberdeen terrier puppy chased the pigeons, barking fiercely, though not in anger. For the puppy it was a game and for the pigeons no more than a passing irritation. Elderly couples sat enjoying the sunshine on the rows of handsome wooden benches, almost all of which had been donated to the city by philanthropists or Scottish regiments or societies or by ordinary families in memory of a relative. A military band had marched along Princes Street a few minutes earlier and the sound of pipes and drums still seemed to echo around the buttresses and crags of the rock on which the castle stood.

Sanderson walked through the gardens, slowly, for he had twenty minutes to waste before his appointment. He sensed that the young woman whom he would shortly be meeting would disapprove if he were to arrive early. Her voice over the telephone had been assured and precise, but without warmth, the voice of a woman who knew exactly what she wanted from life.

When he had answered her call in Maggie's flat in Glasgow, she had said, 'I understand that you met my father, Mr MacNair, a short time ago.'

'Did I?'

'Yes. When you and he were walking in the Highlands.'

'Iain MacNair, the whisky man! Yes, of course!' By then Sanderson had almost forgotten the night he and MacNair had spent in the mountain bothy.

'I'm his daughter, Katriona.'

'I see. How is your father?'

'That's what I wish to talk with you about, Mr Sanderson. Do you think we could meet?'

'Why not? When had you in mind?'

'What about this afternoon?'

The words had been more of a command than a suggestion and Sanderson's instinct had been to resist. 'That's rather short notice, isn't it?'

'You're not working, are you?'

The remark had clearly not been intended to be insolent, but Sanderson was still sensitive on the matter of his redundancy. He edged his reply with sarcasm. 'No, but even the unemployed have commitments.'

'What I wish to talk to you about,' Miss MacNair had replied calmly, 'is urgent. My father has disappeared.'

It had only been then that Sanderson had remembered how Iain MacNair had told him that his life was in danger. Since their meeting in the bothy he had thought more than once of their conversation and had ended by concluding that MacNair's claim had been no more than the fear of too vivid an imagination. The collision with the lorry could have been misjudgement and rock falls were common enough in the Highlands. There were signs by the roadside warning motorists to watch out for them. After hearing his daughter say that MacNair had disappeared, he had wondered whether he should tell her of that conversation, but had decided against it, at least over the telephone.

'I see,' he had replied. 'In that case where would you like us to meet and at what time?'

The meeting had been arranged for that afternoon in the office of the Edinburgh solicitors for whom Miss MacNair apparently worked. Sanderson had travelled from Glasgow by train, for he did not care for motorway driving and he had heard in any case that it was difficult to park a car in the New Town in Edinburgh. Now, leaving the gardens and crossing Princes Street, he found the offices of Balfour, Young and Strachan in what had once been an elegant town house at the far end of Charlotte Square.

Katriona MacNair had an office on the first floor which had been constructed by dividing a much larger room into three and which with its very high ceilings and broad windows seemed narrow and restricted, although it was spacious enough and tastefully furnished. She was smaller than Sanderson had expected, probably in her late twenties, with reddish-brown hair, pleasant enough features and a good many freckles. One had the impression that she was not a girl who laughed very often.

'Did you come to Edinburgh by train?' she asked Sanderson as soon as he had sat down facing her across the desk, and when he admitted that he had she added, 'I must reimburse you for your fare. How much was it?'

'That isn't necessary.'

'I insist. You came here at my request and to suit my convenience.' She opened a drawer in her desk and took out a cash-box.

'No. Forget it please!'

'Mr Sanderson,' she said slowly and deliberately, 'please don't argue with me. Ours has to be a business relationship.'

Sanderson was tempted to observe that he was not aware that they were going to have a relationship, but he decided there was no point in provoking a quarrel. When he told her how much the return fare to Edinburgh had cost she said, 'You travelled first-class, then?'

There was no more than a hint of criticism in the remark. Sanderson had bought a first-class ticket without thinking. First-class travel on trains and planes was one of the luxuries to which he had grown accustomed as a management consultant.

'Yes,' he replied, 'I'm afraid I did.' And when she counted out the pound notes from her cash-box and handed them to him he could not resist adding flippantly, 'Isn't there a subsistence allowance as well?'

'You would have had to eat whether you came to Edinburgh or not,' she pointed out sharply.

'That was supposed to be a joke.'

She locked the cash-box and returned it to the desk drawer without looking at him, as though she were having difficulty in restraining her irritation. Things had started badly, Sanderson reflected, and it would need tact and diplomacy to handle this solemn young woman.

'As I told you on the 'phone,' she said, 'my father has disappeared.'

'When did you see him last?'

'He was meant to be having dinner with me last Thursday but he never turned up. After waiting for an hour I 'phoned him at his home but there was no reply. Next morning I called again and the woman who cleans for him answered. She hadn't seen him and told me she thought he could not have spent the night at home.'

'Perhaps he has been called away unexpectedly on business,' Sanderson suggested.

'It's a coincidence you should think that,' Katriona replied, 'for when I rang his office later that day his secretary said he had gone to Northern Ireland on business. She told me she had booked him on the car ferry from Stranraer to Larne and that he would be away at least until the weekend.'

'But he has still not returned?'

'That by itself would not worry me. But I 'phoned the hotel in Belfast at which he was supposed to be staying and was told he had never checked in.'

'Could he have changed his mind and gone to another hotel or decided to stay with friends?'

'I'm certain of one thing. If my father had been called away suddenly he would have rung me or sent a telegram to say he couldn't make dinner.'

'One would have thought so,' Sanderson agreed, but without conviction. He remembered MacNair as a man of changing moods, susceptible to sudden impulses and therefore likely to be unreliable.

'I can understand your not believing me,' Katriona said acidly. 'So I'd better tell you about our family background. My father would not have missed dining with me that day for the world. If need be he would have postponed his business trip. He'd not seen me for almost ten years.'

She told Sanderson that her mother and father had separated while she was still at school, her father moving out of the family home in Drymen, near Glasgow. Soon afterwards her mother had remarried and Katriona had lived with her and her second husband until she left university and began practising as a solicitor. Now she had her own apartment in Edinburgh.

'And you never saw your father at all during the ten years?'

'No, because I declined to. It was only a week or two ago that I discovered how much I had misjudged and wronged him. So I wrote suggesting that we meet and that he should have dinner with me.'

'And he agreed?'

'He found the letter waiting for him when he returned from his hill walking. He rang me at once to say how thrilled he was. My father is something of a sentimentalist, you understand. Then he followed the 'phone call with a long letter.'

'In which he mentioned meeting me?'

'Precisely.'

Throughout their conversation Katriona's manner had been calm and aloof. Even when she touched on the relationship between her father and mother she had spoken objectively, recounting what she had to say in the precise, dispassionate style and tone of a solicitor in court describing events that had led up to some minor criminal offence. Sanderson found himself wondering whether the detached manner had been deliberately cultivated to create an impression of professional competence or whether it might be a defence.

'What makes you believe I can help you?' he asked her.

'Let me ask you a question first, Mr Sanderson. Why do you suppose my father mentioned you in his letter to me?'

'I've no idea.'

'That struck me as odd. And why did he give me your 'phone number? Could it be that he had a presentiment of danger and was suggesting that if anything should happen to him I should speak to you about it?'

'You're not suggesting that I might be involved in his disappearance?'

She did not answer the question directly. 'He spoke highly of you; said he hoped that one day you might join his company. But perhaps you know something that I don't know. Perhaps he told you something that night in the bothy which might explain why he has vanished.'

The logic and the intelligence of her deduction impressed Sanderson. On the train coming from Glasgow he had debated with himself on whether or not he should tell MacNair's daughter of the fears her father had expressed for his own safety. He still inclined to believe that the car accident and the falling rock were no more than chance incidents and that there was no point in frightening Katriona with talk of attempted murder. But now he realized that Katriona was unlikely either to be easily frightened or to be satisfied with evasions.

'Your father told me that he believed someone was trying to have him killed.'

'Did he say who it was and why?'

27

'No.'

'Tell me what he said.'

Briefly Sanderson told her of the car crash and of how her father had narrowly escaped being killed by a falling rock. Katriona listened without making any comment but he noticed that from time to time she jotted a note on a sheet of paper lying on the blotter in front of her. A shaft of late-evening sunlight slanting through one of the windows fell across her face and neck, highlighting the red in her hair. She was wearing a dark-green costume with a white blouse. The blouse, Sanderson decided, should have been the colour of her hair or an even brighter red. As it was her outfit seemed sombre and masculine.

'Perhaps his fears were just of his imagining,' Katriona said when Sanderson had finished. 'But what you have said leaves me with no option. I have to find out whether anything has happened to him.'

'How will you go about it?'

She looked at him squarely, almost as though she were already defending what she was about to propose. 'I'm hoping that you would act for me; that you would do what has to be done in that direction.'

'Me?' he asked incredulously. 'Why me?'

'One reason is that you have the time and I have not,' she replied, and then before he could interrupt she went on, 'I work in a busy practice, Mr Sanderson, and my diary is even fuller than usual for the next few days. You, on the other hand — and I do not mean to be offensive — are through no fault of your own presently a free agent.'

'I'm looking for a job. That takes time, you know.'

'I'm sure it does, but it should not take very long to establish what has happened to my father; a few 'phone calls, a visit to my father's company, perhaps even a trip to Belfast. And my second reason for asking you to do this is, though one hates to admit it, that men can handle enquiries of this nature more easily.'

She appeared confident that he would agree to her suggestion. It struck Sanderson that she could scarcely have chosen a less gracious way of asking a man to do her a favour. One might have expected an appeal to his good nature, a little charm, perhaps even a smile. Instead of resenting her manner, he was amused.

'It goes without saying that I'll pay you for your time,' she added, and he wondered whether she had guessed what he was thinking.

'If I were to agree, I would not expect payment.'

'And I would not allow you to accept unless you were paid. It has to be a business proposition.'

'So you wish to hire me as you would a private detective?'

'You may look at it that way if you wish, though I would expect a higher standard of service. We employ detectives from time to time in the office and I have no very high opinion of them. And you'd be paid at twice the rate that we would pay a private detective.'

Although he would have been interested to know exactly what that rate would be, Sanderson could not bring himself to ask her. The severance pay he had been given by Macro Consultants had been generous, but recently he had been becoming aware of how quickly one's bank balance seemed to diminish when all transactions were on the debit side.

'If you're inhibited by any old-fashioned reluctance to take money from a woman, you can forget it,' Katriona said. 'I will not be paying you. We have a family trust and the trustees have already agreed to meet any expenses that may be incurred in finding my father.'

'If I agree to tackle this it will be because I liked your father,' Sanderson said. He had already decided that he would do what she was asking without really knowing why, but it was true that he had taken a liking to MacNair that night in the bothy.

'I understand.' Katriona's tone made it clear that she did not believe him.

'You'll need to give me some facts about your father; his home address, the address of his company and so on.'

'I've already written down all you need to know.'

She handed him a sheet of paper which she took from another drawer of her desk. On it were typed MacNair's full name, his home address and telephone number, the address and 'phone number of the Loch Rannoch Whisky Company, the name of the hotel in Belfast where he was supposed to have stayed and the sailing time of the ferry on which he had been booked. Finally at the bottom of the sheet were the address and telephone number of Katriona's flat in Edinburgh.

That she should have already assumed he would be ready to help her irritated Sanderson and he could not resist a sarcastic rejoinder. 'Is that all?'

29

'No.' She reached in her desk drawer again. 'I've made you out a check as an advance on your fee.'

'Bruce, you're crazy, old chap! Absolutely crazy!'

'Simon's right. You were daft to take this job on,' Maggie said. 'What made you do it?'

Sanderson shrugged his shoulders for he did not know the answer. 'It will help fill in idle hours in between interviews for a job.'

'This Katriona MacNair must be a right raver to have conned you into it,' Simon remarked. 'Sexy is she? Big knockers? I know your type, old son.'

'Don't be so pathetic!' Maggie said sourly. 'Not everyone is as obsessed with sex as you are, Simon.'

'You're just jealous because Bruce is a tit man and all your charms are in that lovely little arse of yours.'

Maggie was clearing the table, collecting the plates and knives they had used to eat their cheese and Simon slapped her on the bottom, maliciously and hard, it seemed to Bruce. He had arrived home late for dinner and more than a little drunk. Maggie spat a mild obscenity at him and carried the dishes into the kitchen.

Since he had returned to Scotland, Sanderson had been staying at the flat which Maggie had bought a couple of years ago in a tall, gloomy house just off Queen Margaret Drive and not far from the B.B.C. Besides writing features for the *Glasgow Chronicle*, she did occasional interviews on television as a freelance. She and Sanderson had been good friends at university and had kept in touch in the casual, irregular but good-natured manner of true friends ever since. Simon was supposed to be living with Maggie, but that was an irregular arrangement as well and they fought a good deal, more often than not over Simon's stream of short-lived adventures with other women.

'If you can't be more tactful, you two will end up having another flaming row,' Sanderson remarked to Simon when they were alone. He had heard the two of them shouting at each other late into the previous night.

'Very probably.'

'Why do you bait her so?'

'I don't know.' Simon shook his head gloomily. Then after a

moment's thought he added, 'Do you think it's psychological? Perhaps it satisfies my repressed masculinity to hurt her. On the other hand, perhaps I just want to be shot of her.'

'I can't imagine why.'

'Oh, it's fine for you! You and Maggie are friends. You don't have the word "relationship" always pointed at you like a trident.'

'A trident?'

'Was it not a trident and a net that the Roman gladiators used?' One of the claims made by the expensive public school to which Simon had been sent in England, was that it gave all its pupils a good grounding in the classics. 'Have you any idea how often Maggie asks me, "Do we have a relationship?" in that belligerent voice she has cultivated for her blasted interviews on the box? And every time it makes me want to puke.'

'Why do you find it so offensive?'

'A relationship? What the bloody hell does she mean? Of course we have a relationship, although it may not be the kind of relationship she wants. The poor cow doesn't realize that what her subconscious is saying is, "Why haven't you offered to marry me?". Can't she see that?'

'Does that mean you don't wish to marry her?'

'If I asked her, she'd shit herself laughing,' Simon replied moodily. 'That's the irony. Maggie's always banging on about how she despises marriage. It's all part of the cult.'

Before he could explain what he meant by the cult, Maggie came back into the room, noisily, as though she suspected they might be talking about her and had no wish to hear what they might be saying. The three of them left the dining-table and moved to more comfortable chairs while they drank the coffee she had brought them. Simon fetched a bottle of Macallan malt whisky and three glasses from a sideboard to drink with their coffee.

'How do you plan to start finding this character, Bruce?' Maggie asked as she was pouring the coffee.

'I thought I might go to the place where he works first of all.'

'The whisky company?'

'Yes. Apparently they have offices and a bond in Cumbernauld. I should be able to establish whether he did in fact go to Belfast as he was

31

supposed to have done. If he didn't I'll go to Bridge of Allan, where he has a house, and ask round among his neighbours. Someone must have seen him. A man can't just disappear.'

'Don't you believe it! People disappear every day.'

'I'd also like to know if there was any truth in that tale he told me.' Sanderson had already described to Maggie how MacNair had believed that somebody was trying to kill him. 'If his car was wrecked the way he said, the police would know.'

'Only if he reported that accident. He might have chosen not to.'

'Then at least a motor company would have been called to fetch the pieces. And people living in the neighbourhood would have seen the wreckage by the roadside the following day.'

'I can find out whether the police know anything,' Maggie said.

'Would you do that? Thanks.'

'Surely. Our reporters have good contacts in the Glasgow police. I'll get them on to it tomorrow.'

Simon reached for the whisky bottle and refilled his glass which was already empty. He had contributed nothing to the conversation and seemed scarcely to be listening to what the other two were saying, but sat drinking silently and recklessly. Sanderson wondered whether he was deliberately working himself up into the drunken hostility he needed to provoke a row with Maggie.

'Did you choose this malt whisky?' he asked Simon. 'If so I congratulate you.'

'Twelve-year-old Macallan,' Simon replied, almost wearily, as though the question bored him. 'Matured in sherry wood.'

'Surely an appreciation of whisky was not on the curriculum of your Sassenach education?' Maggie's fine sarcasm showed that her earlier ill temper had not entirely evaporated.

'I should know a little about the stuff. Our bank has enough money invested in it.'

'Christ! Don't tell me that you devious money-lenders have got your hands on our whisky as well!'

Maggie might have forgiven Simon for being educated in England and even for having lost his Scottish accent, had he not chosen when he returned to Scotland to work in the Glasgow office of a London firm of merchant bankers. She had been a belligerent Scottish Nationalist at university and traces of her old passion still lingered.

'Without the banks whisky companies could never survive. Who else could they find to fund all those millions of gallons they hold in their warehouses?'

Sanderson held his glass up to the light. 'It's a fine dram anyway,' he said, trying to deflect the quarrel which he could see was impending.

'Too good for women. Too good to be adulterated with lemonade.' Both of Simon's remarks were calculated gibes. Maggie had always been strong on women's rights and like so many of her sex in Scotland she often took her Scotch with lemonade.

'My God, Simon! You're becoming a middle-aged sexist bore!'

'Middle-aged? Then I must have aged a good deal since six this evening. A little dolly girl I met earlier seemed to find me young enough.'

'So that's why you were late for dinner!'

'Her hands were all over me and she seemed to like what she felt,' Simon said lazily, and then he added spitefully, 'and she was not much more than half your age.'

'In that case why don't you go and spend the night with her, if you think you could manage to satisfy her?'

'If you don't mind I think I will. I took the precaution of memorizing her 'phone number.' Simon rose unsteadily to his feet and moved in the direction of the telephone.

'Don't you dare call her from my flat, you rotten bastard!' Maggie screamed at him.

'Just as you please.'

Changing course, Simon lurched towards the door. Picking up a heavy glass ashtray from the coffee table beside her, Maggie hurled it at him. It struck the wall near the door, shattered and fell to the floor. As he left the room Simon did not even bother to look round.

'Jesus Christ!' Maggie's face was white, her hands trembling. 'One of these days I'll murder that bloody sod.'

## 4

'BELIEVE ME, Mr Sanderson, we are as mystified as Iain's daughter must be.'

'Then you've had no news of him?'

'Not a word since the day he left for Belfast. It's almost a week now.'

Although Peter Wandercliff could not have been far short of sixty, one guessed that he must spend a great deal of money with unisex hairdressers and trendy tailors trying to conceal the fact. His grey hair had been styled in a manner usually popular among much younger men and he wore a beige suit and highly polished brown slip-on shoes with gold buckles. His English was faultless but his accent was almost too perfect, an accent acquired only after years of careful imitation and practice.

'As Miss MacNair may have told you,' he continued, 'Iain never checked in at the hotel in Belfast where a room had been reserved for him, nor as far as we know did he keep any business appointments.'

'Are you sure he left Scotland?'

'I understand he was due to drive down to Stranraer from his home first thing. They tell me his car is not at his house, so we must assume that he did go.'

'When I met him in the Highlands, he told me his car had been wrecked in an accident.'

'That's his own car; a very old, almost vintage Bentley tourer. He loves it and uses it whenever he can. The Volvo is a company car for him to use on business.'

'What do you know about the accident in the Bentley?'

'Not much, except that it happened when he was driving home from a dinner party.'

'Do you know where it happened?'

'On the road from Drymen to Stirling.'

'Are you sure of that?'

'Quite sure. I was at the same dinner party and saw him drive off.'

'Mr MacNair told me that the driver of the goods vehicle which hit his car didn't stop. Have you any idea why that might be?'

'One can think of several reasons. But ask yourself what a juggernaut was doing on a country road at that time of night. My guess is that the driver had been knocking it back in some village pub and was sneaking down to the Clyde by a roundabout route to avoid meeting the police.'

Sanderson hesitated before putting his next question, uncertain if MacNair had meant what he told him in the mountain bothy to be in confidence. Then he suppressed his scruples. 'Mr MacNair believed that the driver of the juggernaut had run into him deliberately.'

'Good God!' Wandercliff exclaimed incredulously.

'He thought someone was trying to have him killed. Do you think that's possible?'

'Did he say why?'

'Not really.'

Wandercliff seemed embarrassed and paused, as though wondering how he should phrase what he was about to say. 'Look, Mr Sanderson. I don't mean this unkindly but I find it wiser not to take everything that Iain says too seriously. Recently he has developed something of a persecution complex.'

'In what way?'

'Ever since the brewers fired him, he started to imagine that everyone was against him. Did you not sense that when you met him?'

'All I can say is that he certainly is very grateful to you for taking him into your company.'

'Grateful? To me?' Wandercliff laughed. 'The boot's on the other foot, believe me. Since Iain joined us our turnover has doubled and that's no exaggeration.'

Wandercliff explained that since MacNair had joined the Loch Rannoch Whisky Company, the labels of all the blends it produced carried the words 'The Finest Scotch Whisky, selected and blended in Scotland by Iain MacNair'. Because the name MacNair was associated with one of the best known Scotches in the world, some of its prestige rubbed off on to the private-label brands produced by the company for its customers. Orders had multiplied, particularly from

35

supermarket chains in Europe which now provided the company with a growing proportion of its business.

'Didn't the brewery which owns MacNair's former company and the brand of that name complain?'

'They did, loudly. But the agreement they made with Iain when they paid him off was not as watertight as they had imagined. He only undertook not to set up another whisky firm marketing a brand under his name.'

'That was careless of them.'

'Very. They tell me the man in the brewery's legal department who drew up the agreement was fired. Anyway you can see the result around you. Before Iain joined me all our bottling was done for us under contract by one of the other bonds. Now we've built our own.'

'That must have meant a hefty capital investment.'

'Yes, but we managed to raise the money between us. When Iain came in he put money into the company and we increased our share capital.'

'You must have a lot of capital tied up in stocks of maturing whisky as well.'

'Not really. Because of the slowing down in world demand there's a good deal of surplus mature whisky around and we've been buying it cheaply, but Iain is keen to change that and build up stocks.' Answering Sanderson's questions seemed to be making Wandercliff restless and he stood up. 'Look, why don't I show you round? As a management consultant you might find it interesting.'

'All right. I'd like that.'

By comparison with the huge blending and bottling complexes that had been built in recent years around Glasgow and Edinburgh by major whisky firms, Wandercliff's bond was modest in size. Behind the office block a long, single-storey building not unlike an aircraft hangar but divided into sections and painted a dull brown, housed all the operations. Following Wandercliff through the sliding metal doors at one end of the building, Sanderson found himself in the blending hall. Casks of whisky stood in rows waiting to be emptied into metal-lined blending troughs set in the concrete floor. Stencilled in white paint on the end of each cask was the name of the distillery from which the whisky came, the year in which it had been distilled and the amount the cask had contained when it had been originally filled and then checked by the Customs and Excise officer. Sanderson noticed that the casks carried the names of several different distilleries, most of which were unknown to him.

'How many different whiskies do you use in your blend?' he asked Wandercliff.

'In our house blend, Loch Rannoch, twelve malts and two grain whiskies. For our private label blends it varies.'

'Do you make a special blend for each customer?'

'God no! That would be quite impractical. Some of the orders are for only a few dozen cases a year. No, we have three standard private label blends. When we are approached by a new customer, we send him samples of all three and he chooses the one he wants. And he knows the whisky he gets is not exclusive, only the label.'

Crossing the hall they watched the casks being disgorged into one of the blending troughs. The casks had been positioned ready in a line astride the trough and the bungs had been withdrawn. Now they were simply rolled over in turn by two men and the whisky gushed into the trough and flowed along into a receiving vessel from which it was pumped into glass-lined blending vats. Inside the vats the blend was thoroughly roused by compressed air and a little caramel might be added to bring the colour up to standard.

'Whisky, like all distilled spirits, is colourless when it comes from the still,' Wandercliff explained. 'It extracts some colour from the wood of the cask in which it is matured and the colour will vary according to the type of cask. After, say, ten years in a cask that formerly held sherry, it could be the colour of rich amber. Whisky matured in reused casks might be very pale. But the customer expects the brand he drinks always to look the same and so a little caramel is added to bring each batch up to a standard colour.'

'How long is whisky left to mature before it is blended and bottled?' Sanderson asked.

'That can vary. Most standard brands are from four to five years old. Single malts and de luxe blends are usually a good deal older; seven, ten or twelve years and often even more.'

Beyond the blending hall and separated from it by a metal partition wall was the section of the building in which the whisky was bottled.

There were three bottling lines of semi-automatic machinery, operated and supervised entirely by women. The whisky was pumped in from the blending vats in glass pipes and after being filtered was filled into bottles which then travelled along the lines being capped with metal closures and then labelled before they reached the end of the line where they were packed into fibre-board cases. Canned music from loudspeakers in the roof of the hall was only partially successful in drowning the incessant clatter of glass against glass as the bottles rattled their way along the lines. Along one side of the hall were small glass-fronted offices for the supervisory staff and the Customs and Excise officers who were there to monitor and check on every drop of whisky that entered and left the premises.

At the end of the bottling lines the cases were sealed and then taken by forklift trucks into a storage area beyond. Sanderson saw that the three lines were filling different brands of whisky, two of them into standard full-sized bottles and the third into flask-shaped half bottles. In the cased goods store were many other brands, stacked in piles of varying sizes.

'Where is all this whisky shipped?' he asked Wandercliff.

'To different export markets.'

'Do you sell any in the home trade?'

'No. The home market is monopolized by the big companies.'

Sanderson knew that what he was saying was not strictly true. He had tasted some of the 'own label' brands of Scotch put out by supermarket chains, most of them in his view whisky of poor quality and probably not more than three years old.

As they were walking back to the office block he remarked, 'When we met in the Highlands, Mr MacNair mentioned that he was working on two new ideas that would transform the whole whisky trade.'

'Really? Did he say what they were?'

'No. I thought you might know.'

'Since Iain joined me I've left the production side entirely to him.' Wandercliff smiled boyishly. 'And to be frank, Mr Sanderson, I've had other things on my mind for the past few months. I only returned from a world cruise a short time ago.'

'Could you not hazard a guess as to what this new idea might be?'

'I'm really in the dark, I assure you. Iain has a small lab in the office block where he messes about with whisky samples. He won't even allow me in the place because I use after-shave which makes it impossible, so he says, to nose samples accurately. And did you notice that a small area of the blending hall has been partitioned off?' Sanderson had to confess that he had not noticed this and Wandercliff continued, 'That was Iain's doing. He has the door kept locked at all times and a notice on it to the effect that there is strictly no admission except on his authority.'

'Have you not asked him what he keeps in there?'

'Never. Why should I? I've every confidence in Iain and to tell you the truth I've no great interest in the scientific aspects of whisky production.'

They had arrived back at the office block and went into Wandercliff's office. Sanderson had noticed earlier, as he had sat facing Wandercliff, that there was a silver photo frame on the desk and now, as they came into the room, he could see that it held a portrait photograph of a very beautiful woman, whose face seemed vaguely familiar. Wandercliff went to a cabinet under the bookshelves and took out a cut-glass decanter of whisky and two glasses. As Sanderson knew, it was the custom in the whisky trade if the time of day was appropriate, to offer all visitors a dram. As Wandercliff was pouring, a woman who, Sanderson guessed, must be his secretary, came into the office.

'What is it, Mrs Hastie?'

'I had no wish to disturb you, sir, but I thought you should know that the police telephoned while you were out in the bond.'

'What did they want?'

'They've had a message from the constabulary in Northern Ireland.'

'Mr Iain has turned up?'

'No, but his car has been found abandoned in a wood some miles outside Belfast.'

Sanderson had not been in the bar of the Albany hotel more than a minute or two when Simon arrived, surprising him for he had not supposed that Simon would bother too much about punctuality. He had telephoned him at his office earlier in the afternoon suggesting that they should meet for a drink that evening and chose the Albany rather than Maggie's place because he was uncertain whether the quarrel which had erupted the previous night might still be smouldering. Maggie's moods, he had learned, were a great deal more unpredictable than they had been in their university days, and often tinged with bitterness.

Simon had the look of a man who had not yet recovered from the ravages of a night of dissipation. He was fingering an ugly, purple bruise on his lower lip tenderly. Sanderson bought him a large gin and tonic and a whisky for himself.

'You look as though you need this,' he remarked as he handed Simon the glass.

'I've never made up my mind whether women bite because they enjoy it or because they believe it's a proof of passion,' Simon said gloomily. 'You should see my neck and shoulders. That girl has teeth like a piraña. Silly little cow!'

'Then there really was a girl waiting for you last night?'

'Of course!'

'I thought you might have invented her just to annoy Maggie.'

'What sort of shit do you think I am?' Simon demanded indignantly. In his moral code pretending to be unfaithful was more reprehensible than infidelity itself.

'Are you going to patch up last night's little difference of opinion?'

'I suppose so. What I should really do is to get out of her life altogether. We're not suited; not suited at all. You're the kind of chap she really hankers for, Bruce.'

'Me? Maggie has never had any interest in me!'

'That's only because all her life she has chased after not what she really wants but what she thinks she should want.'

'Next you'll be telling me I can give her the relationship she needs.' Remembering their conversation the previous evening Sanderson could not resist teasing Simon.

'Don't you fancy her?'

'I did when we were adolescents, but that's all over.'

Their university days were not embedded so deeply in the past that Sanderson could not remember the anguish of his feelings for Maggie; anguish because she had been either unaware of or indifferent to what he felt for her and because she would confide in him, describing in painful detail her romances with a succession of other men, mainly macho rugby-playing undergraduates. Now he could look back at those days and at the rebuffs and at his hurt pride without emotion. It was all over.

'Maggie didn't ask you to speak to me, did she?' Simon asked with sudden suspicion as he bought them both another drink. 'A dove of peace? She expects me to apologize, I suppose.'

'This has nothing to do with Maggie. I asked you here to pick your brains.'

'Pretty meagre pickings, old son. What can a poor bank clerk tell a whiz-kid consultant?'

'Let's talk about whisky. It's big business is it not?'

'Enormous. The growth rate over the past twenty years has been staggering.'

For a man whose main interest in life appeared to be girls, racing and gin, Simon knew a remarkable number of facts about the whisky industry. He threw a few of them out, casually. World sales of Scotch, Sanderson learned, had more than quadrupled in not much more than twenty years and it was now exported to more than 180 countries throughout the world, earning more than £800 million. At times the value of the stocks of whisky maturing in Scotland was greater than the country's gold reserves.

'How many companies are there in the industry?' he asked.

'About fifteen reasonably large firms, a slightly larger number of medium-sized ones and a whole shoal of minnows.'

'How would the Loch Rannoch Whisky Company rank?'

'Your missing friend's outfit? It used to be a minnow but it's growing rapidly. Must be a clever old stick, that Dutchman!'

'Dutchman?'

'Wandercliff. Came over from Amsterdam, they tell me, where his name was Van de Cleef. Started a small broking business at a time when mature whisky was in short supply and one could make a decent living out of broking. Then he moved into producing and exporting in a small way and then wham! Suddenly his business explodes, he builds his own bond and starts supplying the largest chain of hypermarkets in France.'

41

'Wandercliff says it all began when MacNair joined him.'

'It's possible, I suppose, but I would have thought there's more to it than that. Anyone can get into the whisky business in a tiny way. All one needs is the use of a 'phone and a few contacts. But to move into the big time you need money; a lot of bread, boy! And however much capital you may have, you must get the banks behind you. As I said last night, it's the banks who keep the industry going.'

'MacNair's name and reputation must have helped there.'

'Christ!' Simon exclaimed suddenly. He was sitting facing the doorway and as he looked over Sanderson's shoulder his face clouded with irritation. 'So it was a set-up!'

Sanderson turned round and saw Maggie coming into the bar. 'What the hell is she doing here? I didn't tell her I was meeting you, Simon, I promise you.'

Maggie walked up to them, kissed Simon on the cheek as he stood up and laid a hand on Sanderson's arm. She had recorded a television interview that afternoon with a visiting pop singer which had gone well, and she looked pleased with herself.

'How did you know we were here?' Sanderson asked.

'I didn't. I'm having dinner with my agent. He thinks he may be able to fix me up with a television chat programme.'

She pointed towards a far corner of the room where a young man in a brown corduroy suit was sitting on his own. He waved at her. 'By the way, Bruce,' she said, 'I've news for you. The police have no record of an accident being reported by any Iain MacNair. But they do say that about the time you were in the Highlands an articulated road vehicle was stolen from a lorry park on the outskirts of Glasgow.'

'Stolen?'

'Well, driven away. It was found the following day, abandoned near the Erskine Bridge. And it was badly damaged in the front as though it had been in a collision.'

## 5

THE BODY HAD been washed up on the foreshore at Luce Bay in the parish of Glasserton. A farm worker named Gilmour had seen it floating in shallow water, being first washed in to ground on the sand and then towed back as the waves retreated. He had dragged it up on to the shore and then, seeing that the man was dead and past any help, gone to the farmhouse to telephone the police.

Superintendent Long of the Dumfries and Galloway Constabulary had heard the news of the body's discovery with patient resignation. A less philosophical man might have felt aggrieved, for no other police force in Scotland had been plagued by a succession of bodies, unwanted and mainly unidentified, coming out of the sea. What still mildly astonished him was that the appearance of so many corpses on a small stretch of Scotland's coastline should have aroused so little public interest. The *Dumfries and Galloway Standard* had made the most of the story and the Glasgow papers had printed a brief report of each discovery, but no hordes of reporters and photographers and no television crews had arrived in the little town of Stranraer to stand around drinking in the hotel bars and to pester him with questions. Long did not want publicity for himself, but a few headlines in the nationals and a story on the box at peak viewing time might well have brought forward people who could identify the bodies.

He was a tidy man and having a string of unexplained deaths on his files offended his sense of tidiness. Over the last ten years, excluding the one which had been found that day, no less than seven bodies had been washed up out of the sea in his district and none of the deaths had yet been explained. Five of the corpses had not even been claimed or identified. They had come with monotonous regularity and some-times in moments of gloom Long wondered whether this might not be a visitation, the sea giving up its dead as a grisly reminder of mortality, a warning to the folk of Scotland for the decline in public morality which Long saw all around him, gambling, fornication, murder and even drinking on the Sabbath. On the other hand, staunch and unforgiving Presbyterian though he was, he had to concede that Stranraer had been corrupted by the sins of the flesh far less than other parts of Scotland. The town was not a tourist centre, too far south of Rabbie Burns country, and even the Northern Irish who came swarming over on the ferries from Larne had scarcely disturbed its sleepy charm. There was little to cause the police any bother, except the bodies.

Any number of theories had been put forward to explain why so many of them had been washed ashore in the district. Experts had studied the tides and currents in the sea, but had been unable to find any common factor which might explain from where and by what route the bodies had arrived. One suggestion was that all the bodies were those of victims of sectarian violence in Northern Ireland, conveniently disposed of by being dropped into the sea off the coast, but since the majority had been women that seemed unlikely. Another odd fact, hard to explain, was that all the women appeared to have come from the middle classes. What puzzled Long most was that in spite of all the enquiries which the police had made in Britain and Northern Ireland, the bodies had not been identified. He knew that most missing persons who remained missing were those who chose to disappear. Given a reasonable description, particularly in the case of a woman, the police more often than not soon heard of someone missing from a district or in circumstances which would allow one to conclude that she was the corpse, even when a positive identification was physically impossible.

Today, when he went out to the body in Luce Bay, Long decided there was more than an average chance that this one would be identified, even though it was without clothes. The middle-aged man had clearly been in good physical shape and had sound teeth with a gold inlay, tidy hair and well-kept fingernails. He was no vagrant but a man who had looked after himself. Moreover, there was a long jagged scar on the right arm running from wrist to elbow. This one, Long was certain, would be recognized and claimed as soon as a description had been circulated.

44

Even so he was surprised when as early as that afternoon he had a telephone call from Glasgow asking for details of the body that had been found in his district that morning. 'How did you know about the body?' Long asked the man who had called.

'A friend of mine works on the *Glasgow Chronicle*. The story was 'phoned in by their stringer in Stranraer.'

'I see. And may I ask what your interest in this matter is, sir?'

'My name is Sanderson. A friend of mine, a Mr Iain MacNair, has been missing for some days.'

'Can you describe him please, sir?'

Sanderson described MacNair's appearance as accurately as he could. When Maggie had called him from the *Chronicle* that morning to tell him about the body in Luce Bay she had mentioned the bodies that had been found in the district earlier and that at least one of them was thought to have fallen from a ship leaving Northern Ireland. It seemed a slender connection but worth a telephone call to Stranraer.

'The general description fits that of the deceased,' Long said cautiously when Sanderson had finished, 'but it would fit hundreds of men. Do you know if your friend had a gold filling in his teeth?'

'No, I can't say.'

'How well did you know this Mr MacNair, sir?' Long was beginning to wonder about Sanderson. A faint suspicion that he might be a journalist crossed his mind. He could see no reason why, if the man was a reporter, he should not admit the fact, but journalists were apt to try all sorts of tricks.

'Not very well. I only met him once, but his daughter, who stays in Edinburgh, asked me if I could find out what has happened to him.'

'I see.'

Sanderson could sense Long's suspicion, not so much in what he said but in the silence that followed, crackling like static electricity. He said, 'Miss MacNair has not seen her father for several years and I was with him only a few days ago.' Then, sensing that what he had said was totally inadequate as an explanation for the questions he was asking, he added, 'And she is a busy lawyer who does not have the time to look for him herself.'

'Are there any other next of kin, do you know, sir?'

'Only Mr MacNair's former wife as far as I know. She has remarried and lives in Drymen, I understand.'

'We will be needing someone to identify the body, or rather to ascertain if it's that of your friend.'

'Should I 'phone Miss MacNair and ask her to come?'

'My advice would be to say nothing to her at this stage, sir. You would distress her unnecessarily if the body proves to be not that of her father.'

'Then what do you suggest?'

'Could you spare the time to come to Stranraer yourself, sir? Just as a preliminary measure.' Long was anxious to meet this young man who was busying himself in the affairs of people whom he appeared to know only very slightly.

'Why not? If it would help I could drive down to you now.'

'That would be very kind of you, sir. Come to the police station and ask for me. Long is my name.'

On the tedious drive from Glasgow to Stranraer, Sanderson wondered how much, if anything, he should charge Katriona MacNair as expenses for the journey. Part of the deal he had made with Macro Consultants when he left the company was that he should be allowed to buy the car with which they had provided him for business use at a nominal price. The car was a Mercedes 280 SL, basically a two-seater and not designed for business purposes, but he had chosen it as wholly suited to the image he had been trying to project, that of a dynamic young bachelor with expensive tastes. On the road to Stranraer the Merc, as always, had swallowed petrol extravagantly and Sanderson felt certain that even if he were to charge Katriona for just the cost of the petrol, she would suspect that he was loading the bill. He decided it would be more tactful to charge her the price of a return rail ticket, but first-class, of course.

As he drove he began to regret agreeing to Superintendent Long's suggestion that he should go and look at the body which the sea had washed up in his district. Once before he had been asked to identify dead bodies and the memory of the experience still disturbed him. The bodies had been those of his mother and father, both killed outright when their car had skidded in heavy rain on the narrow, winding road that ran along Loch Lomond and had crashed into an

46

oncoming bus. They had not been mutilated too savagely in the accident but he could still picture his father's head sagging on a broken neck and the frozen grimace of fear on his mother's face.

When he reached Stranraer, Long asked him more questions. Some were about the circumstances in which MacNair had disappeared, but an equal number were about how Sanderson had met him and about the enquiries he had so far made. The Superintendent was courteous enough, but with the canniness of a true Scot he still had doubts and intended to double check the answers he had been given earlier on the telephone.

As they walked through to the mortuary attached to the station, Sanderson decided it was his turn to ask questions. He was curious to know whether the police had any convincing explanation for the otherwise bizarre series of coincidences that had brought a succession of bodies to their shore. Long admitted that they were still baffled and told him of the efforts they had made to solve the puzzle. He talked freely about the affair as he always did, reasoning that the more widely the facts were known the greater the chance of someone coming forward to identify at least some of the bodies.

When they reached the mortuary and were taken into the room where the body lay, Sanderson had to steel himself to look at it. Some decomposition of the features had already begun to set in as a result of immersion in water, but if he had felt any doubt the distinctive scar on the right forearm would have convinced him.

'I'm afraid there's no doubt in my mind,' he told Long. 'It is Iain MacNair.'

Katriona's flat was in the New Town, that part of Edinburgh which, in spite of its name, was not new at all but one of the earliest and best examples of town planning, a network of broad streets between which Georgian houses were grouped in squares or crescents around small gardens of trees and grass, a plan in which Adam had played a major part. Looking at the houses, splendid in their proportions but grey and sombre, Sanderson wondered why, now that Edinburgh was free of smoke and soot, the city fathers did not promulgate an edict that all householders must clean the exterior stonework of the buildings and so return them to their original beauty.

The door to the first-floor flat was opened by a small blonde girl with an athletic figure. She must have been about the same age as Katriona but was a good deal less reserved in manner and she welcomed Sanderson with the eager curiosity of a collector presented with a new and unusual specimen.

'Kate,' she called out as she led him into the drawing-room, 'here's a man asking for you. Where have you been hiding him, that's what I'd like to know.'

Katriona, who was sitting reading what looked like a file of correspondence, did not seem to be amused by her friend's levity. She introduced the girl as Gillian Masters.

'Offer the man a drink, for goodness sake!' Gillian said, and turning to Sanderson she added, 'We have whisky, gin and a bottle of dreadful Cyprus sherry.'

'Whisky will be fine, thanks.'

'Mr Sanderson is here on business.'

'That's no reason for not offering him a little traditional hospitality.'

Sanderson took the drink that Gillian poured him and sat down. After pouring two more, a whisky for herself and a gin and tonic for Katriona, she moved towards the door, 'Next time come earlier,' she said before leaving the room, 'in time for dinner. If you're lucky it will be my turn to cook. Kate's no cordon bleu, I can tell you.'

When they were alone Katriona said to Sanderson, 'You have news for me, I assume.'

'Yes, and not very good news, I'm afraid. That is why I came in person rather than 'phoning.'

'My father's dead, isn't he?'

'Yes.' Trying to soften the blow would be pointless, Sanderson decided. 'His body was found on the shore near Stranraer this morning.'

Katriona looked away and did not speak for several seconds. It was the only sign of emotion that she gave. When she did speak her voice was controlled as always. 'Had he drowned?'

'They won't know until the autopsy has been performed. In my view it's not very likely.'

Sanderson explained that MacNair's body had been naked when it

48

was found. Had he fallen into the sea accidentally and drowned he would certainly have still been wearing at least some of his clothes. Although the police had not detected any obvious wounds on the body which might have been caused by a gunshot or a knife, it was not unreasonable to believe that he had been killed and the body thrown into the sea in an attempt to dispose of it. Weeks, even months might have passed before it was found or it might never have been recovered at all.

'Then my father was right when he told you that somebody was trying to have him killed.'

'It seems so. I also learned today of evidence which suggests that someone stole a transport vehicle and used it to ram your father's car in the way he described to me.'

'Do you know where that happened?'

'Yes. On the road from Drymen to Stirling. Your father was driving home from a dinner party given by your mother.'

Katriona was about to make a comment but then she seemed to change her mind and bit her lip instead. Chewing her lip was a habit of hers Sanderson had noticed and she did it in a way which distorted what at other times was an attractive mouth. He supposed it might be a nervous habit, except that she had never shown any other signs of nerves.

'So I've completed what you asked me to do,' he said after a pause. 'I'm only sorry that I had to bring you such melancholy news.'

'You can hardly say that you have done what I asked,' Katriona replied firmly. 'I wanted to know what had happened to my father and all you've told me is that he's dead; nothing about how he came to be killed and by whom.'

'You're not suggesting that I should attempt to find that out?'

'Indeed I am. And why not?'

'That's a matter for the police, surely?'

Katriona made a small, contemptuous noise. 'I've no very high opinion of the police, Mr Sanderson. Have you any idea how many unsolved murders there are in Scotland each year?'

'I wouldn't know where to start.'

'Have you a notion at all why anyone should have wished to kill my father?'

'When we spoke up in the Highlands he seemed to imply that it may have been on account of some new idea he was developing in his business.'

'Then why don't you start at his home?'

'His home?'

Katriona explained that after his marriage had broken up MacNair had gone to live in Bridge of Allan. If he was so secretive about the new idea he was developing as his conversation with Sanderson indicated, then, Katriona suggested, he would probably have kept all the information and details of the idea at his home rather than in his office at the Loch Rannoch Whisky Company. Sanderson could see the logic in her suggestion.

'Why not go to Bridge of Allan and take a look around my father's house? You may find something there which will give an indication of what he was doing and of what other people may have been involved.'

'Can I do that? I've no authority to search his house.'

'A woman goes in every day to clean for him. A Mrs Duncan. I'll 'phone her and explain that you have my permission to look round the house. You may learn something from her as well.'

With some reluctance Sanderson agreed. He was finding that Katriona, in spite of her uncompromising manner, was a difficult girl to refuse. 'I'll drive up there tomorrow. Can you give me directions to find the house?'

Once again Katriona appeared to hesitate. Then she said abruptly, 'No, I'm afraid not. I've never been there.'

# 6

MRS DUNCAN WAS a small, neat woman, a typical wee Scottish wifey, well-mannered and polite but with a natural reserve which a stranger might reasonably mistake for suspicion, even hostility. Sanderson could feel her giving him a visual third-degree interrogation as they talked in the doorway of MacNair's house.

Had it not been hidden by trees, the house itself would have looked incongruous among the substantial, grey middle-class houses on the wooded hillside overlooking Bridge of Allan. It was a bungalow, built in the shape of an L and almost Mediterranean in flavour, with its white walls, green window shutters and pink tiled roof. Unexpectedly in so modern a house it had an open fireplace and the chimney had been given a small pagoda-shaped roof similar to the chimneys above the kiln in a malt whisky distillery, a little fantasy of MacNair's and not the architect's, Sanderson decided.

'It is a dreadful thing! Dreadful!' Mrs Duncan exclaimed. She had learned from Katriona on the telephone that morning of her employer's death. 'And him such a fine, braw man! Who would wish to harm him, that's what I'm asking myself.'

'So far as you know he had no enemies?'

'Enemies? Never! Everybody liked the man.'

'Did he spend much time at home, Mrs Duncan?' Sanderson asked. He was not certain what questions he should be asking the woman or whether she could possibly give any answers that might help him.

'Not as much as he should have done. He worked far too hard, poor soul; at the office until all hours and at the weekends and on holidays he would be working here, typing letters, reading books and journals. Sometimes he even brought samples of whisky back here with him.'

'What did he do with the samples?'

'How should I know? Duncan and I have never let a drop of the stuff pass our lips, nor did our parents, nor have our children.'

Sanderson realized that Mrs Duncan and her husband belonged to the ranks of those righteous, church-going and sometimes puritanical Scots who were opposed to drinking as a matter of principle. His own parents, although by no means regular drinkers, had been liberal in their views but his upbringing in the Highlands had made him aware at an early age of the sharp polarization in the attitudes of the Scots to strong drink. Those who were opposed to alcohol, secure in the knowledge that they had the authority of the Church of Scotland behind them, never concealed their disapproval of those who indulged in it, while Scots who enjoyed a dram treated teetotallers with ribald scorn. Whole communities, even families could be bitterly divided over drink and drinking. He wondered why, if she felt like that, Mrs Duncan should have come to work for MacNair, and then realized that in a small village like Bridge of Allan there would be little alternative work for a woman who no doubt needed the money.

'I was told you believe that Mr MacNair did not sleep here the night before he went to Belfast,' he said.

'He did not.'

'How can you be so certain?'

'Because his bed was still made, his bedroom tidy and not even a dirty cup and saucer in the kitchen for me to wash the next morning. Orderly and methodical though he was in his work, Mr Iain was not a tidy man, poor soul. And one thing more. I'll not believe he ever went to Northern Ireland.'

'Why is that?'

'He took no luggage with him, not even an overnight bag. Whenever he went away on business Mr Iain took a change of clothing and his shaving kit with him at least.'

'Are you sure he took nothing?'

'Aye, I'm sure enough. All his luggage is still in the house and his toiletries.'

Sanderson did not press the matter. A man might decide to make a business trip at short notice and not have time to go home and pack. It would not be hard to buy a razor and a clean shirt. He allowed Mrs

Duncan to show him round the house. In one arm of the L were two large bedrooms, each with its own bathroom, a smaller, single bedroom and a shower room combined with a sauna; in the other a large living-room, a study and a kitchen.

As he looked into each room in turn, Sanderson saw nothing that was likely to throw any light on MacNair's death. All of them were comfortably furnished but curiously anonymous, perhaps because they seemed to contain so few personal belongings; no photographs, no trophies, not more than a handful of books, no souvenirs or mementos. One felt that MacNair, having had a house designed precisely to suit his present and likely future needs, had made no more than a token attempt to turn it into a home. Even the study appeared to be no more than an extension of his office at the whisky company.

Even so, the study must be the room that was most likely to offer some scrap of information which might explain why the dead man had thought his life to be in danger. In addition to a writing desk, it was equipped with one of the latest models of electronic typewriters and a filing cabinet with three compartments. Lying on the desk was a tiny microcassette tape recorder of the type overworked businessmen were encouraged to use for dictation and in a drawer of the desk he found several unused miniature cassettes.

After Mrs Duncan had left him to continue her household chores, he began his search. On the desk itself, apart from a tray full of ballpoint pens, paper clips, a stapler and a bottle of the fluid used to paint over typing errors, he found only a pile of wine and spirit trade journals; the *Morning Advertiser, Harper's Wine and Spirit Gazette,* the *Scottish Licensed Trade Guardian* and *La Revue Vinicole.* Flicking through them Sanderson found nothing of any interest. No passages had been marked or underlined in any of the journals, nor had any items been cut out. The drawers of the desk were unlocked but they were equally unrewarding, empty except for a few sheets of notepaper embossed with MacNair's home address, letter paper printed with the logo and address of the Loch Rannoch Scotch Whisky Company, envelopes and a supply of plain typing paper.

Sanderson turned his attention to the filing cabinet and to his surprise when he pulled on the handle of the top drawer, it slid open easily. For a man as secretive as MacNair to have left the cabinet unlocked seemed a most uncharacteristic lapse unless it held nothing of any importance. All the files in the top drawer appeared to contain correspondence and other items of a personal or family nature. One was full of bank statements, receipts, invitations to dinners and cards confirming appointments with dentists and doctors. Another held sketches and drawings of MacNair's house and correspondence with the architect and building contractors who had designed and built it. There were other files for insurance policies, correspondence with his solicitors and with garages and another in which all the weekly payments he had made to Mrs Duncan were methodically recorded.

The second drawer down of the cabinet was also unlocked and the first file which Sanderson drew out of it was labelled:

MATURATION OF WHISKY
1. Correspondence with government departments.

Inside it, arranged in datal order were letters which MacNair had received over a period of almost eighteen months. Sanderson drew out the top letter and read it.

Ministry of Agriculture, Fisheries and Food,
Whitehall Place, London SW1A 2HA.
01-233-3000

Your Ref: 1DM/SW/1
Dear Mr MacNair,
Thank you for your letter of 3 February in which you suggest that H.M. Government should initiate action which would remove the requirement for Scotch whisky to be matured.

You are no doubt aware that the requirement for whisky to be matured is laid down in the definition of whisky found in Paragraph 1 of Schedule 7 to the Finance Act 1969 (as amended by the Finance Act 1980) which stipulates inter alia that the expression 'whisky' or 'whiskey' shall mean spirits which have been matured in wooden casks in warehouses for a period of at least three years.

Removal of the requirement to mature whisky would thus entail amending the definition in a future Finance Act. This, as I am sure you will appreciate, would come within the province of the

54

Treasury and would more particularly be the responsibility of H.M. Customs and Excise.

May I respectfully suggest, therefore, that in the first instance you should write to the Customs and Excise, setting out in detail your reasons for advocating a change in the definition of whisky.

Yours faithfully,

J. Bashworth-Hunt.

There was no copy of MacNair's letter to the Ministry of Agriculture, nor of any other letters he must subsequently have written on the subject. Sanderson decided that this must have been because MacNair had been an inexpert typist and too lazy to make carbon copies of what he had typed. As if to confirm this theory, there were no sheets of carbon paper in the desk drawers. It meant that Sanderson would have to deduce what MacNair had written from the replies he had received and he wished that the man might at least have had photocopies made of his letters before he sent them.

Evidently he had followed the Ministry of Agriculture's advice and written to the Customs and Excise, for the next letter in the file had come to MacNair on headed paper from King's Beam House, the head office of that government department. It acknowledged a letter from MacNair and said that the writer would be obliged if, in order that his request might be given full consideration, MacNair would state why he believed the change in the definition of whisky which he was suggesting would be to the advantage of both the consumer and the whisky industry. The letter concluded with a warning:

I feel I should say I believe it is unlikely that the Government would be prepared to make such a fundamental change unless it had the support of the whisky industry as a whole. As you may know, when in the past it has been suggested that the period of maturation for whisky should be reduced, this has always been opposed by the industry.

The next three letters in the file, spaced over a period of almost three months, were all from the Customs and Excise. The first thanked MacNair for his second letter and stated that his proposals would be

55

given careful consideration, but that before reaching a decision the Customs and Excise was obliged to consult the Ministry of Agriculture as the sponsoring ministry of the whisky industry and through it The Scotch Whisky Association and all other bodies which might have an interest in the matter. The second and third letters had clearly been written in response to complaints by MacNair and gave elaborate, implausible reasons for the length of time which the process of consultation was taking.

It was clear to Sanderson as he read the correspondence, that the civil servants were simply going through the motions of considering MacNair's proposals and that they were less than enthusiastic about them. The inescapable conclusion was that eventually, after several months and innumerable letters between all those concerned, the proposals would be politely rejected.

MacNair, too, must have realized that he was making no progress with the civil servants, for he had begun writing to other people, trying to enlist their support for what had become his crusade. The file contained letters addressed to him from Members of Parliament, including the members for the constituencies in which both his house and office were situated, as well as from the Scottish Director of the Confederation of British Industry and the General Secretary of the Scottish Trades Union Congress. All of them were replies to letters which MacNair had written and none of them were in any way helpful.

The last letter in the file, written only a few weeks previously, was also from the Customs and Excise and in it the writer assured MacNair that his proposals were still under active consideration. Sanderson could only wonder whether the civil servants had deliberately been dragging their feet, prolonging the affair in the hope that MacNair would eventually lose heart and lose interest. The second file in the drawer was labelled:

MATURATION OF WHISKY — 2. General

In it Sanderson found a miscellaneous collection of documents, tables cut from trade journals which gave the prices of new whisky from all the distilleries in Scotland, a copy of a paper on maturation given at a scientific conference, a faded clipping from a newspaper report that a

56

Japanese inventor had discovered a way of accelerating the maturation of whisky, a letter from Pentlands Scotch Whisky Research Ltd, giving analyses of two samples of whisky that MacNair had evidently sent them. Another letter which caught Sanderson's eye as he flicked through the file was from the manager of Glen Cromach distillery. It informed MacNair that two hogsheads, one containing new whisky which had been filled to his order the previous week and one cask, number 8506, from a parcel of whisky owned by the Loch Rannoch Whisky Company, had been sent under bond by road transport to Cumbernauld in accordance with his instructions.

There were only two files in the middle drawer of the cabinet, the space at the back of the drawer being taken up by empty bottles of the type used for storing whisky samples. When Sanderson opened the bottom drawer he found it contained a number of files, all of them marked simply with the letters S.O.S. and all of them empty.

He slid the drawer shut thoughtfully. The cabinet was of the type in which all the drawers were locked simultaneously by pushing in a cylindrical metal plunger on one side of the top drawer. The plunger activated a vertical bar inside the cabinet which slid into place, holding all three drawers firmly shut. To open them again one needed the key which fitted into a keyhole on the plunger and which when turned released the plunger and the locking bar.

Pulling out the top drawer and peering into the cabinet, Sanderson could see that the locking bar was badly twisted. He examined the edges of the top drawer carefully and saw an indentation in the metal, caused in all probability by some kind of instrument being slid in between the drawer and the body of the cabinet. An attempt had been made to repair the damage by straightening the buckled metal, but there was no doubt in his mind that cabinet had been forcibly opened.

He found Mrs Duncan in the kitchen, polishing the tiled floor with an electric polisher and asked her, 'Has anyone been to the house since Mr MacNair left?'

'Not as I know of. Why?'

'The filing cabinet in the study is unlocked and I believe it was forced open.'

'Then someone must have been in the house. Mr Iain was very

particular about keeping that cabinet locked at all times.'

'Does anyone else have a key to the house?'

Mrs Duncan shook her head. 'No, but this explains something which puzzled me. The other morning I found a letter lying on the floor of the study to one side of the cabinet. It could not have been there the morning before, because I cleaned the carpet with the vacuum cleaner that day. I thought at the time that perhaps Mr Iain had been back to the house, maybe to collect some papers.'

'Do you have the letter?'

Mrs Duncan fetched the letter which, she explained, she had put away in a drawer of MacNair's dressing table for safekeeping. It was addressed to MacNair, written in longhand but on the printed stationery of the Strathclyde Linen Bank. The address of the letter head was that of the bank's head office in Glasgow and, neatly printed below the heading, were the words 'From the Chairman'.

'When did you find this?' Sanderson asked Mrs Duncan.

Her brow wrinkled with the concentration of trying to remember, for one day was much like another to Mrs Duncan. 'Three days ago; no, the day before yesterday. Yes, that's right, the day before yesterday.'

'Then it would not have been dropped by Mr MacNair.'

'Yes, we know that now.'

'Are you sure no one else has a key to the house? His secretary at the office perhaps?'

'No. Whoever broke into the cabinet must have broken into the house as well.'

## 7

MAGGIE'S WAS A second-floor flat and when Sanderson arrived back from Bridge of Allan and was climbing the stairs, he met a man coming down. The man stopped and looked at him enquiringly.

'Would you be Sanderson?' he asked.

'Yes.'

'I'm here to see you.'

The man's manner was so direct and blunt that Sanderson wondered for a moment whether he was a sheriff's officer come to serve a writ. His build too, short and powerful but paunchy, would have matched many people's preconceived stereotype of a sheriff's officer or bailiff. On the other hand he was expensively dressed and in any event Sanderson had done nothing to earn a writ.

'What do you want to see me about?' he asked the man.

'About Iain MacNair. I'm Jock Ferguson.'

'Oh yes?'

'I'm married to Iain's ex-wife Brenda.' Ferguson seemed irritated at having to explain his connection with MacNair. 'I'd have thought you knew that.'

'Shall we go upstairs?'

'There's a young woman there. We can't talk in front of her.'

'We could go to the pub across the road?'

'My club would be better. My car's outside and Joe will bring you back here afterwards.'

When he had arrived at the house Sanderson had noticed a red Jaguar parked by the pavement a short distance away with a uniformed chauffeur sitting at the wheel. He had also noticed that the car registration number was JAF 1. For a car owner to buy a registration number — and usually the price to be paid was absurd — which corresponded with his initials had always struck him as a piece of pretentiousness which bordered on the ridiculous.

'We can get a decent dram at the club,' Ferguson added, implying that the brands of Scotch whisky likely to be available in Sanderson's local pub would not suit a discriminating drinker.

'All right.'

They were driven into the city in the Jaguar and the chauffeur pulled up outside the entrance to the Midas Club just off Blythswood Square. Like most people in Glasgow, Sanderson had heard of the Midas Club but had never been invited to visit it. Modelled on the traditional men's clubs of London, it had been started a few years previously by a group of Glasgow businessmen who, it was said, had been rejected when applying for membership of the more exclusive Western Club. The Midas had the advantage of being housed in a new building designed for the purpose, but had even so aped the old-fashioned style of London clubs, with a porters' desk just inside the entrance and club servants wearing morning dress. Unlike London clubs it also had a commissionaire in a blue and gold uniform whose sole function appeared to be opening the doors of the chauffeur-driven cars in which the club members arrived.

'We'll not go in the bar. Too many of my friends will be there,' Ferguson said, seemingly oblivious of how offensive the remark might seem to his guest. 'Come to the smoking-room.'

In the smoking-room, as everywhere in the club, the walls and ceilings were painted blue and gold with gold predominating, as if as a reminder of the club's name. The deep leather-covered armchairs and the rows of leather-bound volumes in the bookshelves looked out of place in a modern room that was all concrete and glass. They sat in two of the chairs by a huge picture window which gave them contrasting views of Glasgow traffic. Immediately below them a green double-decker bus crawled up one of the hills on which the city was built followed by a string of cars, while more distantly one could see lorries and more cars hurrying at 60 miles per hour above the roof tops on the elevated motorway, their drivers relieved, no doubt, at not having to enter the city at all.

After shouting at one of the club servants to bring them two large whiskies, Ferguson lit a cigar. He took his time, as though he were wondering how best he could start what he had to say. But finesse was not his style and after a moment he asked Sanderson brusquely, 'What's your interest in Katriona?'

'Interest?'

'Are you a private investigator?'

'Certainly not!'

'Then as you've been going around asking questions about what happened to Iain, you must be doing it for Katriona.'

'How did you find out that I've been looking for her father?' Sanderson had no intention of allowing Ferguson to thrust him on the defensive with a string of questions.

'My wife spoke to the police at Stranraer.'

'Did she go and identify his body?'

'No. Iain's partner drove down to Stranraer yesterday evening.'

'Then there's no doubt that it was his body?'

'None.'

'The answer to your original question,' Sanderson said, 'is that I have no interest in Miss MacNair, just a business arrangement.'

He told Ferguson briefly of how he had met MacNair while hill walking and of how Katriona had asked him to see whether he could find out what had happened to her father. Ferguson listened in a way which suggested that he had not made up his mind whether to believe what he was being told. He sat untidily in his armchair, his fat thighs well apart and his suit, charcoal grey with an exaggerated chalk stripe, although obviously made to measure, hung on him uncomfortably.

'And what have you found out?' he asked when Sanderson had finished.

'Nothing that you don't already know.'

'You saw his body. Had he been murdered?'

'I couldn't possibly say and the police are not committing themselves until an autopsy has been carried out.'

'You may be wondering why I and not my wife came to see you,' Ferguson remarked inconsequentially. He appeared to find it difficult to pursue any firm line of questioning, possibly because he wished to conceal his motives in asking the questions or because he personally was not interested in the answers to them.

'Your wife asked you to?'

61

'Yes. She's too upset by what happened to Iain to see anyone. Brenda's still very fond of Iain, in spite of the way he treated her.'

'He didn't strike me as the kind of man who would maltreat a woman.'

'Brenda had a bloody terrible life when they were together. Of course, Iain didn't have much money then.' Ferguson paused, meaningfully, and then added, 'His cash came later.'

'Are you saying he was wealthy?'

'Loaded, the lucky bastard! What a golden handshake he got when the brewers fired him!'

'He was entitled to compensation after the way they treated him.'

'Maybe, but he kept it dark all right. Brenda only found out how much he collected a wee while back. Did Katriona no mention it?' Ferguson looked sly as he grinned and added, 'I wonder why.'

'She may have not thought it was important.'

'Iain should have given some of it to Brenda. She's the one who deserves compensation after the life he led her. But she got nothing, even though Iain lashed out six grand to pay some idiot's debts.'

'Whose debts?'

Ferguson shrugged his shoulders. 'Some man who was fired by the brewery company not long after they gave Iain the push,' he replied. Then he switched the direction of the conversation again. 'Have you met Iain's partner?'

'Once, but that was before he knew that Mr MacNair was dead.'

'He'll need to get down to work again, now Iain's not there to run the business. That won't suit him.'

'Why do you say that?'

'He's besotted with that girl,' Ferguson said scornfully and then added an obscenity which meant the same thing, before concluding, 'Lady Jane Dornoch.'

Sanderson remembered the photograph he had seen on the desk in Wandercliff's office and knew now why the face of the girl had seemed so familiar. Jane Dornoch, the younger daughter of the Earl of Tain, was better known in London society than in Scotland. Often seen in fashionable discothèques and a companion of younger members of the Royal Family, she had been rewarded with the supreme accolade of frequent mentions in the William Hickey column. Her beauty was almost as stunning as her father's poverty and inebriety, but even so there had once been talk of a royal marriage for her.

'He's twice her age and been married twice before.'

'Then why did she marry him?'

'Are you joking? The bleeding earl, her dad, is broke and Wandercliff's not short of a bob or two. They say he made a million in five years after he came to this country.'

'He's good-looking too and young for his age.' Sanderson was driven to defend Wandercliff by his irritation at Ferguson's spite.

'If I'm any judge the girl's no good in bed. I give the marriage two years.'

'How long have they been married anyway?'

'Only a matter of months and it's been one long honeymoon. He hardly ever leaves her side.' Ferguson repeated his crude description of Wandercliff's state of mind.

'Did he bring her to the dinner party which you and your wife held in your house?'

'What party was that?'

'The one the night a juggernaut rammed Mr MacNair's car as he was driving home.'

It may have been Sanderson's imagination but Ferguson's manner seemed to change. Although he still sat slumped in his chair, he was suddenly alert and watchful, but he said nothing.

Sanderson repeated his question. 'Was Mrs Wandercliff at the dinner party?'

'Lady Jane. Aye and why not? Half the bloody top drawer of Glasgow were there.'

'You sound as though you didn't enjoy it.'

'It was the cost of the dinner that got up my tits. Claret at eighteen quid a bottle!' The expression on Ferguson's face suggested that he had probably quarrelled with his wife over the cost of the dinner. 'And these titled folk who haven't got fourpence to their name, were guzzling it down as though they never drank anything else.'

'Who else was there?' Sanderson had a premoniton that his question was going to produce an interesting answer.

'Lord and Lady Muir. He's Jane's half-brother. Oh aye, and the chairman of the Strathclyde Linen Bank, Sir Douglass Tweedie.'

\*　　\*　　\*

63

After refusing an invitation to lunch at the Midas Club and making his escape from Ferguson, Sanderson had a beer and a pie in the first pub he came to and then made his way to the nearest branch of the Glasgow City Public Library. The first part of the research he wished to do did not take long. The current edition of *Who's Who* told him that Sir Douglass Tweedie had been born in Aberdeen, was sixty-two years old and a widower who had been given his knighthood in the Birthday Honours three years previously. He also learned that Sir Douglass, beside being chairman of the Strathclyde Linen Bank, was a non-executive director of Scottish and International Distillers p.l.c., one of the largest companies in the Scotch whisky business.

On an irrational impulse Sanderson had taken the letter from Sir Douglass to Iain MacNair which Mrs Duncan had found and brought it with him from Bridge of Allan. Now he read it again.

Dear Iain,
I ran into Bill Waterton the other day and your name came up in conversation, which reminded me that it is a long time since we last met. This must be your fault for working so hard! In the old days I could always count on seeing you at the N.B. lunch, the Benevolent or the 49 Club meetings, but recently, as they say, you have been conspicuous by your absence.

It so happens there are one or two matters relating to the Trust which you set up for your girl that I would like to discuss, so why not come and lunch with me at the Western Club one day next week? Get your secretary to 'phone my Miss Kilgour and arrange it.
Yours aye,
Douglass.

The date on the letter showed that it must have been written about three weeks before MacNair had gone hill walking in the Highlands. After making a note of the telephone number of Sir Douglass's office, Sanderson put the letter away and began his second piece of research, which was to learn all he could about the maturation of whisky.

Surprisingly it proved to be a subject on which he could find little precise or scientific information, even in any of the several books on

64

the production of Scotch whisky in the library and Sanderson had to piece together such slender facts as he could collect from reference books and trade journals.

He already knew from the correspondence in MacNair's files that whisky had to be matured for a minimum of three years in casks made from oak, but he did not know why and in what way this period of maturation improved the whisky. Almost all of the authors writing on the production of whisky admitted quite frankly that while dramatic changes certainly did take place in the flavour and character of the spirit as it lay in the cask, the scientific reasons for these changes were not fully understood. The wood from which the casks were made was porous and this allowed a process of slow evaporation which in some way removed the harsher, more fiery constituents in new whisky and left it smooth and mellow. Maturation must thus be an expensive process, Sanderson realized, for some of the whisky was also lost by evaporation, about two per cent each year according to books which he read.

Another fact which surprised him was that the legal requirement to mature whisky dated back only to the First World War. Lloyd George, the Prime Minister at that time, had been responsible. Believing that drunkenness among munition workers had been the reason why armament factories were failing to supply the guns and shells which the army needed in the quantities and to the standards required, he had hit on the idea of limiting available supplies of whisky by introducing legislation preventing it from being sold until it had been matured for two years. Another measure he took was to limit the hours during which alcoholic drinks could be sold. Historians had later shown that he had been wrong in blaming the failings of the munitions industry on drink and that bad management and inadequate training for workers had been the real cause, but the legislation requiring whisky to be matured had never been repealed.

The trade journals in the library revealed that because of the remarkable growth in world sales of Scotch during the three decades that followed the Second World War and a slowing down in that growth during the recent recession, the stocks of whisky now maturing in Scotland amounted to more than 3,000 million litres of pure alcohol. Litres of pure alcohol, the basis of official statistics, meant nothing to Sanderson, but using a pocket calculator he worked out that this volume of whisky was the equivalent of at least 9,000 million bottles. Because of this surplus, the editor of one journal complained, mature whisky could now be purchased too cheaply and as a result large numbers of poor-quality brands were being shipped to export markets to the detriment of the image of Scotch.

On leaving the library, Sanderson found that the evening papers were being sold in the streets and he bought a copy. The story of the body washed up in Luce Bay, which had been given only an obscure paragraph in the morning editions, had now been promoted to a more prominent position and given a headline.

### WHISKY MAN'S BODY FOUND ON BEACH

Yet another body, the eighth in ten years, has been washed up on the Solway coast to baffle the police in Dumfries and Galloway. This time it is a mystery with a difference, for while the other bodies were never identified, this one, it has been established, was that of Iain MacNair, for many years a leading figure in the whisky trade and a director of the Loch Rannoch Whisky Company. What puzzles the police is how MacNair's naked body came to be in the sea. He disappeared a few days ago after leaving home to travel to Northern Ireland on the ferry from Stranraer. He never arrived at the hotel where a room had been reserved for him and his car was later found abandoned in a wood outside Belfast. The cause of MacNair's death has not yet been confirmed but foul play is suspected and the police are working on a theory that he may have been the innocent victim of yet another sectarian killing in Belfast, mistaken for another man.

The report went on to tell readers of Iain MacNair's background and family, that he lived alone in Bridge of Allan and that his former wife was now married to a well-known Glasgow businessman, Jock Ferguson. Mrs Brenda Ferguson had been interviewed by a reporter from the *Evening Times* but had been unable to give any possible reason why her former husband might have been murdered.

Sanderson took a taxi back to Maggie's flat and from there telephoned the head office of the Strathclyde Linen Bank. When he asked the switchboard girl if he could speak to Sir Douglass Tweedie she replied, 'May I know who's calling?'

Evidently Sanderson's name failed to impress her for she put him through not to Sir Douglass but to his secretary, a Miss Kilgour, who answered in a young, brisk voice. She explained that Sir Douglass was in a meeting and could not be disturbed.

'Then I'll ring back,' Sanderson said.

'May I know what it is you wish to speak to him about?'

'I would like to make an appointment to see Sir Douglass, tomorrow if possible.'

'It's not likely that Sir Douglass could manage that. He has a very full diary tomorrow.'

Sanderson decided he would have to be more aggressive if he were to penetrate the defensive network of telephonists and secretaries which protected the chairman of an important bank. 'Would it help if I told you I wished to speak to Sir Douglass about Mr MacNair?'

'Mr Iain MacNair?'

'Yes. You will see from the evening papers that his dead body has been found on the beach in Luce Bay.'

Miss Kilgour paused, trying to decide how best to deal with this unusual situation. People often telephoned demanding appointments with Sir Douglass, but in the main they were disgruntled customers of the bank. Sanderson's request sounded to her like blackmail. Finally she suggested, 'Why not give me your 'phone number, Mr Sanderson? I'll see if I can have a word with Sir Douglass and ring you back shortly.'

Sanderson did as she asked and put the telephone down. In less than five minutes it rang and Miss Kilgour was on the line. 'Mr Sanderson? I've spoken to Sir Douglass and he will see you at twelve tomorrow. You know where our offices are, I assume?'

## 8

SIR DOUGLASS TWEEDIE looked and very often behaved like a dour Scots accountant. To do so was an undeniable asset in his business and he had found it could also be useful socially, discouraging the small talk of those with whom he did not wish to be bothered, in much the same way as a drab colour or slightly offensive odour protects plants or insects from predators.

In his work as a management consultant, Sanderson had often come face to face with Scots accountants, for it was remarkable how many of them had succeeded in infiltrating English businesses, rising more often than not to positions of authority. Caution, thrift and an incorruptibility based on a Presbyterian upbringing were the virtues for which Scots accountants were noted, but Sanderson was not deceived by Sir Douglass's camouflage and suspected that the man had other qualities which he did not display, flexibility of thought, diplomacy and ample reserves of charm.

'It was good of you to spare the time to see me, sir,' Sanderson said, deciding that if charm were to be deployed, he should be the first to use it.

Sir Douglass looked at him dourly through his rimless spectacles. 'I can give you ten minutes. What is the nature of your business?'

'It's about Mr Iain MacNair.'

'You knew Iain, then?'

'Only slightly.'

'Are you a newspaper reporter?'

'No. Miss Katriona MacNair has asked me to find out what I can about the circumstances of her father's death.'

'Is that so?'

Clearly Sir Douglass had decided not to volunteer any information and to answer any questions which he might be asked in as few words as possible. Sanderson had to think of a way by which he could prise him out of his posture. Charm would not work but perhaps a more aggressive manoeuvre might.

'Have you any idea why Mr MacNair might have been murdered?' he asked.

'It has not yet been established that he was.'

'But if he were?'

'I have no idea whatsoever.'

'Two attempts were made on his life not long before he disappeared. He seemed to believe that they were connected with a new process he had developed.'

Sanderson saw at once that his remark, partly guesswork and partly deduction based on the slender evidence of what MacNair had told him in the mountain bothy, had struck some kind of target. The change in Tweedie's manner was far from dramatic but it was perceptible. The cold, grey eyes still stared through the spectacles but one could sense that they were not now obdurate but defensive.

'New process?'

'Yes. A way of dispensing with the necessity for maturing whisky.'

Sir Douglass seemed to sigh. 'So he told you about that?'

'He had several files of letters and papers on the subject in his home.'

'Mr Sanderson, there is one thing you ought to know,' Sir Douglass said in the manner of a man who was going to be frank, but reluctantly, because he was divulging confidences which he would have preferred to keep to himself. 'I knew Iain MacNair since he was a bairn and I was a close personal friend of his father. For as long as he was with the family firm Iain was a first-rate lad, modest, utterly dependable and a whisky man through and through. But after he fell out with the brewers and left the company, he changed completely; seemed to go right off beam. He began involving himself in all these hare-brained schemes, almost as though he was trying to revenge himself on the industry and on his old friends.'

'Is his process a hare-brained scheme?'

'A way of eliminating the maturation of whisky?' Sir Douglass sniffed contemptuously. 'There's nothing revolutionary about the concept, I can assure you. People have been talking about it and

69

trying out new ideas for years. One might say it's a kind of whisky philosophers' stone. Every now and then somebody announces that he has found the secret, but it's usually nothing more than filtration in one form or another; very often filtering whisky through charcoal.'

'And that doesn't work?' Sanderson asked.

'Filtration will remove some of the undesirable constituents of new whisky. Unfortunately it also removes some of the more desirable elements, those which give Scotch its unique flavour. No, we've been through this all before many times. There's no substitute for maturation. It's an essential part of the process of making Scotch whisky.'

'But what if someone did discover another way of achieving the same result?' Sanderson persisted.

'That would be no reason for having him murdered. The suggestion is absurd.'

Sanderson had been making some calculations, using the figures he had extracted from the books and journals in the public library. As whisky lay in the warehouses maturing its value increased. The amount of the increase would vary according to the type of whisky and the current level of demand for mature whisky, but at a very conservative estimate the value of the stocks of maturing whisky in Scotland at replacement cost must be somewhere between 15,000 and 20,000 million pounds.

'If it became legal to blend, bottle and sell whisky straight from the still,' he told Tweedie, 'that would knock thousands of millions of pounds off the value of Scotland's whisky stocks.'

'You're surely not implying that someone in the whisky business had Iain killed to stop his process being recognized?'

'We're talking about a hell of a lot of money. And most of it is bank money, I understand.'

Surprisingly Sir Douglass did not lose his temper. Instead he laughed. 'My dear man, all this is just fancy! Idle speculation. Even if Iain had discovered a way of producing good whisky without maturation, it would never have been allowed. The Government would never change the law.'

'Why not?'

'Why should they? The whisky industry would be opposed to it and so, as you say, would the banks be. It would benefit no one.'

'What about the consumer? If whisky did not have to be matured it would be less costly to produce.'

'A little less, yes. A few pence a bottle. Most of what you pay for a bottle of Scotch is tax. Eighty per cent of it, in fact. The actual cost of the whisky is very small. And the Government is already under fire by the growing band of do-gooders and the temperance movement for allowing drink to become too cheap and so encouraging alcoholism.'

'Too cheap! Do they know what one has to be pay for a dram in a Glasgow pub?'

'The whole scheme was crazy. As you probably know, Iain had been pestering the Ministry of Agriculture and the Treasury, writing to MPs and to the papers, trying to win support for his idea and he was getting nowhere. He was making a fool of himself. It was sad really.'

'Is that what you told him when you lunched together?'

Tweedie looked at Sanderson sharply, wondering no doubt how he had learned about his invitation to MacNair. 'I tried to persuade him to drop the idea,' he said. 'I felt I owed it to him and to his father.'

'But he didn't listen to you?'

'He scarcely even listened to what I had to say. It was a different Iain from the one I had known for so long; stubborn and defiant.'

'Did you tell him that the Government would never change the legal definition of whisky?'

'I did and I believe he had already come round to accepting that, but it didn't alter his stand. He told me that if the Government refused to act, he had another way of defeating the Establishment. That was the expression he used; the Establishment. I would have thought he was a little old to start behaving like an angry young man.'

'Was he angry?' Sanderson asked.

'What you are really asking is was I. No, Iain didn't lose his temper and nor did I. When I saw he would not be swayed with reason, I decided to drop the subject.'

'And you finished your lunch on good terms?'

'Of course!' The corner of Tweedie's mouth twitched in what his friends would have recognized as a smile. 'You'll not give up this notion of yours, will you Mr Sanderson? You still believe that it was

71

the banks or the distillers who had poor Iain killed.'

'According to statistics the vast majority of murders are motivated by sex or money. Mr MacNair didn't seem to have had any sexual involvements.'

'No, but he had a good deal of money, his own money, I mean.' Sir Douglass looked at his watch, an ancient Omega with a worn, black strap. He did not believe in spending money on personal ornaments. 'I said I could give you ten minutes and we have run out of time. Sorry I cannot be of more help.'

Sanderson accepted the dismissal, thanked Tweedie and left. On his way out he had to pass through the office of the chairman's secretary and there he found Miss Kilgour standing by her desk, ready to go out, it seemed. He wondered whether she had been waiting for him to leave before going to lunch. She had chatted with him familiarly while he had been waiting to see Sir Douglass. Now her manner was even more friendly.

'Are you going down to the ground floor?' she asked him.

'Yes, unless you have any better suggestions.'

'Let's go down first. Then I may have.'

They rode down in the elevator together. Sir Douglass's office was on the top floor of the building and the elevator stopped at every floor on the way down to the vestibule, collecting passengers as it went. Miss Kilgour did not speak during the journey and kept her eyes averted demurely, but when they were in the street outside the entrance to the building she smiled.

'Now I have a suggestion,' she said. 'Why don't you buy me a drink?'

'Why not, indeed? I'd like that.'

His response may not have sounded as enthusiastic as he intended, for Miss Kilgour added, 'As the solicitors say, you may hear something to your advantage.'

'Where would you like to go?'

'Anywhere, but not too close to the office.'

'Have you time for lunch?' Sanderson asked her as he hailed a passing taxi.

'All the time in the world.'

They lunched at the Fountain in Woodside Crescent. Miss

Kilgour put away two large whiskies without difficulty as they studied the menu in the bar. Sanderson indulged his sense of humour by imagining what the austere Katriona MacNair would say if he told her that the expenses he had incurred on her behalf included lunch with an attractive young woman in an up-market restaurant.

'This is my last week with Sir Douglass,' Miss Kilgour remarked as they made their way into the restaurant.

'Why? Are you moving to a better job?'

'Better only in the sense that it will be more bearable. The old shit has fired me.'

'Surely it's impossible to fire a secretary these days unless she actually knees her boss where it hurts most?'

'I only wish I had! No, Sir Douglass always gets what he wants. He's clever and he's devious and in this case what he wanted was not me, if you know what I mean.'

After being liberally helped from almost every dish on a sumptuous hors-d'oeuvre trolley, she managed a huge portion of lamb cooked to an old English recipe, followed by a cluster of profiteroles covered in cream. A psychiatrist, Sanderson supposed, would have diagnosed Miss Kilgour's appetite as a subconscious response to being fired from her job, an attempt to compensate for being rejected and unloved. If that were so, she had been unwise in choosing the lamb, for it was heavily seasoned with old English wild garlic.

Not until she had finished eating and had a coffee and Rusty Nail in front of her, did she decide that she would reward Sanderson. 'Did you know that Iain MacNair came to see Sir Douglass a wee while ago?' she asked.

'I did and I asked Sir Douglass about it.'

'What did he tell you?'

'That he had invited MacNair to lunch in order to persuade him to abandon a secret process on which he was working.'

'A way of cutting out the need to mature whisky.'

'You know about it?'

'Yes. It was supposed to be hush-hush.' Miss Kilgour laughed scornfully. 'But you can't keep secrets from a good secretary. And Douglass has an awful loud voice.'

'Do you know why he was bent on persuading MacNair to drop his scheme?'

'He didn't feel very strongly about it himself. He was confident it would come to nothing and that the civil servants would turn the proposals down, but his friends in the whisky trade asked him to use his influence with Iain MacNair.'

'I gather he was not able to make MacNair change his mind.'

'What did Sir Douglass tell you? That they had agreed to differ and parted good friends?'

'More or less. He said they had finished their lunch on an amiable note.'

Miss Kilgour laughed; a short, staccato laugh, loud enough to have shattered the Fountain's whole stock of glasses had she struck the right note. 'The lying old goat!'

'What did happen?'

'They had a flaming row. I could hear them shouting at each other.'

'Did they indeed?'

'They never went to lunch at all. Iain walked out in a rage.' Miss Kilgour leant back in her chair. She seemed to be savouring the memory of Sir Douglass's rebuff almost as much as she was enjoying the Rusty Nail which she had ordered with her coffee. Then she added with malicious innuendo, 'Of course, the row may not have been over the whisky maturation business at all. Iain also came to see Sir Douglass about a trust which he had set up for his daughter. Sir Douglass is one of the trustees.'

'Who are the other trustees, do you know?'

'There's only one, his partner Peter Wandercliff.'

## 9

THAT AFTERNOON SANDERSON drove out to Cumbernauld. As he stopped his car in the small parking area in front of the office block of the Loch Rannoch Whisky Company, Wandercliff came out of the building and began walking towards a yellow Volvo. He was wearing a pale-blue linen suit, a blue and white Dior tie and white shoes. When he saw Sanderson arriving, he changed direction and came across to him.

'Have you heard about Iain?' he asked.

'Yes. I'm so sorry. What a terrible thing!'

'Shocking! I tried to discourage him from making those business trips to Belfast. He could have handled everything over the 'phone or by letter.'

'Then you believe he was murdered in Ireland?'

'It seems the only possible explanation. And it's a devastating blow for our company, I can tell you. He's irreplaceable, totally irreplaceable!' Wandercliff looked at his watch. 'I've no wish to be discourteous, Bruce, but I was just leaving. Jane is expecting me.'

'That's all right. I really only came to have a word with Mr MacNair's secretary if that's all right by you.'

'Mrs Hastie? Of course. You met her the other day. Iain and I shared a secretary. There's not much letter writing in our business. I know Mrs Hastie will be glad to help in any way she can.' Wandercliff turned to leave and then paused. 'Have you found out anything in the enquiries you've been making?'

'Only what Mr MacNair's secret was. He was working on a way to do away with the maturing of whisky.'

'Ah, now I understand!'

'Understand what?'

'I took a look in that enclosure he had rigged up in the blending hall this morning and found some casks of whisky he had been keeping there. He must have been using them in his experiments.'

'What whisky did he have there?'

'Two hogsheads of Highland Malt, one twelve years old and the other of new whisky.'

'Nothing else?'

'Only a pile of oak chips and a number of filtering devices.'

'Why oak chips, I wonder.'

Wandercliff shrugged his shoulders. 'I've heard that in some European countries oak chips are sometimes put into casks of grape brandy in order to speed up maturation. There's no doubt that both brandy and whisky take some flavour from the wood of the cask while they're maturing and oak chips in the cask would expose the spirit to a greater area of wood.'

'Do you believe MacNair's process might have worked?'

'I really can't say. Iain knew as much about whisky as anyone in the business. Oh yes, I know it's the fashion these days to put young graduates with science degrees in charge of production but Iain knew things that aren't taught at universities. Whisky was in his veins.' Wandercliff held out a hand to shake Sanderson's. 'And now I really must go. Mrs Hastie will look after you.'

Sanderson watched him as he strode away, climbed into his car and drove off. He had always understood that the whisky trade was a tough, competitive business and he wondered how a man with such a casual attitude to his company's affairs could have been so successful as Wandercliff, starting as he had with so few advantages. On the other hand, it might be that Wandercliff's seeming lack of interest was no more than a passing phase, a symptom of his obsession with his young wife, which was also reflected in his bright, trendy clothes.

He went into Mrs Hastie's office and found her engrossed in a long, gossipy conversation with a friend named Rhoda. Much of the talk was about men, and he guessed that Mrs Hastie must be a widow or perhaps divorced and now in the market for another man.

When finally the girlish confidences had been exhausted, she turned to face him. 'Oh, Mr Sanderson, wasn't it sad about poor Mr Iain?'

'Very sad.'

'And him such a nice creature. A real pet! Of course I've only known him since he joined Mr Peter, but he and I got on famously. Whenever I did a specially tricky piece of work for him he would bring me flowers or chocolates.'

'Have you no idea at all of who might have wished him dead?'

'None at all. It must have been some dreadful mistake.'

'He seemed to believe that people in the whisky business were against him.'

'He may have trod on a few toes, but that was mostly jealousy on their part because he and Mr Peter were doing so well.'

'Mr Peter says that Mr MacNair deserves the credit for that.'

'Aye, he does. The company has really begun to take off since he joined us. He was such an efficient organizer, you'll understand, and dedicated to his work. Do you know I came into the office early one day not long ago and found that he had been here since six?'

'What was he doing?'

'Going through all the company's old files and records. It was while Mr Peter was away on his honeymoon cruise. Mr Iain decided he would have all the important documents put on microfilm and to junk the rest. Then he planned to install a computer in the space he saved.'

While they were talking a young girl, a junior clerkess, Sanderson assumed, came in carrying tea on a tray. The tea was served in a pot of fine bone china with a milk jug and two cups and saucers to match. Wandercliff, it seemed, when he adopted the habits of the British, liked to do so in style. Mrs Hastie poured tea for both of them.

'Mrs Hastie, was it you who made the arrangements for Mr Iain's visit to Belfast?'

'Of course. I booked him on the ferry and reserved a room for him at his usual hotel.'

'When did he ask you to do all that?'

'Only the day before he left.'

'Was that not rather short notice?'

'Maybe, but it was by no means the first time that Mr Iain had decided to make a business trip on the spur of the moment. As he lived alone he was a free agent.' There was an undertone of disapproval in the remark, as though Mrs Hastie disliked seeing a good

77

man going to waste when so many women were short of one.

'Perhaps he had a 'phone call from Belfast asking him to go.'

'Maybe. I'm not sure.'

Mrs Hastie explained that the day before he left for Belfast MacNair had not been in the office but in the north of Scotland, visiting distilleries around the valley of the Spey. A very large number of whisky distilleries were concentrated in that part of the country and MacNair would often drive up to Speyside for the day to call on them.

'In the early evening,' she concluded, 'I had a 'phone call from the north asking me to book a place on the Stranraer ferry for the next morning, to reserve a room for him in his usual hotel and to make an afternoon appointment with Mr Driscoll, one of his business contacts in Ireland.'

'Did Mr Iain say why he was going over?'

'I can see I've not made myself clear, Mr Sanderson. I never spoke with Mr Iain that day. A man from the distillery rang to say that Mr Iain had been trying to reach us all afternoon without success. So before he left the distillery he asked them to give me a message just as soon as they could get through. The message was to make all the arrangements for his trip.'

'Which distillery was it?'

Mrs Hastie appeared surprised by the question. 'Do you know, I'm not certain. He was to make four or five calls that day and I never thought to ask who it was who gave the message.'

'Which distilleries was he due to visit?'

'Let me see. Glenturret would be the first for it's on the way north. Then on Speyside he was going to call at Glenfarclas, Tormore, Glen Cromach and Macallan.'

'Was he going to place orders for whisky with all of them?'

'Not necessarily. We've never filled with them before, but Mr Iain was anxious to improve our blends by laying down stocks of the very best malt whiskies. It was just an exploratory visit.'

Sanderson wondered whether MacNair would have told the distilleries of his process to eliminate maturation. They might not have been eager to supply him if they knew of his intentions.

Mrs Hastie continued, 'He also intended to raise another matter at

Glen Cromach. When he was going through our records he found what appeared to be a discrepancy in the cask numbers of some whisky we have at the distillery. It was not a matter of great importance, but he wished to make sure that our inventories were correct.'

'Did you think of checking to make sure the 'phone call was authentic?' Sanderson asked her.

'Why should I? Mr Iain went to Belfast often and whoever gave me the message knew the name of his regular hotel and about Mr Driscoll too.' As the implications of the question seeped into Mrs Hastie's mind her eyes opened wide. 'Are you thinking the message never came from Mr Iain at all? That I was told to make the arrangements so that when he disappeared we'd think he was in Belfast?'

'Very probably.'

'That would mean they had already planned to kill him.'

'Mrs Hastie, by the time you had that call, Mr MacNair might well have already been dead.'

Back at Maggie's place that evening Sanderson glanced through the morning papers to see whether they carried any more reports about the body washed up at Luce Bay. Maggie took all the Glasgow and Edinburgh daily papers and a number of the English ones, believing it was important for both her newspaper work and broadcasting to keep herself well informed. Edinburgh's paper, the *Scotsman*, parochial as always, had given no more space to the death of a Glasgow businessman and the *Glasgow Herald* had contented itself with a paragraph saying that police enquiries were continuing. The English papers seemed unaware of a little domestic incident on the wrong side of the border and only the *Daily Record* carried a follow-up story. They had decided that MacNair had been murdered and, having found out that he had disappeared while on a business trip to Ireland, had decided that it was a sectarian killing. The suggestion was that MacNair had in some unspecified way antagonized the Catholic community in Northern Ireland and that the I.R.A. had been called in to eliminate him. The theory was colourfully presented if not very plausible.

Sanderson was still reading the press reports when the telephone rang and he recognized Katriona's voice. 'I thought you should know,' she said, 'the police from Stranraer called me a short while ago. They have established that my father was murdered. He had been dead some time when his body was put into the sea.'

'I see.' Sanderson hesitated, wondering whether it would be acceptable to ask a girl directly how her father had been murdered.

'He had been strangled.'

'I'm sorry.' As an expression of sympathy the words sounded pitifully inadequate.

'Will it help your enquiries in any way to know that?'

'It confirms what I suspected; that he may have been killed before he disappeared, in all probability the day before he was supposed to have left for Northern Ireland. By tomorrow I hope I shall know exactly how it was arranged.'

'And by whom?'

'No, that's going to be more difficult.'

'You'll keep me informed, won't you?'

'Of course. There's one other thing you might be interested to know. Your step-father came to see me yesterday.'

'My step-father?'

'Jock Ferguson.'

'He's not my step-father,' Katriona said angrily. It was the first time he had heard her sound anything but calm and aloof. 'I was an adult when he married my mother.' She paused and then added, 'What did he want?'

'To tell you the truth I'm still not quite sure.'

'You would be advised not to attach any great credence to what he may have told you.'

'He didn't say much of any significance.'

Katriona did not comment for a time and then she seemed to reach a decision and said reluctantly, 'It might be as well if you and I were to have another meeting, Mr Sanderson. There are things about my family which you should know and which I prefer not to discuss over the telephone.'

'All right.'

'Could you come to Edinburgh tomorrow?'

'Yes, but not until the evening. I plan to drive up to Speyside in the morning.'

'Then come round to my flat in the early evening. I'd offer you dinner but, as Gillian told you, I'm not much of a cook.'

It was the nearest thing to a joke that she had made since he had met her and Sanderson was surprised enough to respond impulsively, 'I've a better idea. Let me take you out to dinner.'

'I don't think so,' she replied but only after hesitating. 'It doesn't seem like a good idea.'

'Why not?' he said persuasively. He was about to add that he would not charge the dinner to his expenses but thought better of it. Instead he said, 'I shall need to eat after travelling all day and it will save you having to cook for yourself.'

'All right then.'

'I'll pick you up at your place at seven-thirty,' he said quickly, not giving her time to change her mind, and put the telephone down.

As he was speaking Maggie came into the room. She had been in the kitchen preparing a meal and now came in to start laying the table. She had overheard the last part of his conversation with Katriona and now she smiled.

'Making a play for the lady solicitor, are we?' she teased.

'That will be the day! But I must find some way of communicating with the girl. This lawyer-client syndrome is driving me spare.'

'Well it saves me having to ask you if you would mind eating out tomorrow evening.'

'So, you want me away! Do I smell intrigue?'

'Simon is coming to supper. We had a long meaningless conversation on the 'phone this afternoon. I think that in his own stiff-lipped, staccato way he was saying that he wants to kiss and make up and he'll do it more easily if we can be alone.'

'Good on you, as they say down under.'

Maggie came over and touched Sanderson lightly on the cheek. 'You don't mind, do you pet? He's coming to supper but to make sure he stays on for breakfast — permanently — is going to need delicacy and finesse.'

'Of course I don't mind. And I'll be out all day so you'll have plenty of time to tart the flat up for the seduction scene.'

'Don't be like that! And where are you off to anyway?'

'To Speyside. I plan to call at a few distilleries.'

'When I was on holiday one year I followed the whisky trail which the tourist board has set up for visiting distilleries. Which ones are you going to?'

Sanderson told her the names which Mrs Hastie had given him. When he had finished Maggie exclaimed, 'Glen Cromach! Now that's a coincidence!'

'Why do you say that?'

'I had never heard the name before and then ten minutes ago I came across it in the evening paper.'

A copy of the Glasgow *Evening Times* lay on the sideboard where Maggie had dropped it when she arrived home earlier in the evening. Picking it up she glanced quickly through the pages.

'Here we are. It's a report of an inquest on a Scot named Fraser who died in Portugal. The verdict was that he died of food poisoning.'

'Haven't a number of tourists died in similar circumstances in Portugal over the last year or two?'

'Yes and no one believes they died of food poisoning. The most likely explanation is that they were killed by gas fumes from faulty installations in new apartments, but that the authorities will not admit it in case it puts tourists off going there.'

'You said it was a coincidence,' Sanderson remarked.

'The coincidence is that this man Fraser was at one time manager of Glen Cromach distillery.'

## 10

THE MORNING WAS crisp and clear. As he sat eating his breakfast in the dining-room of the Foulford Inn, Sanderson looked out over the fields which lay on the far side of the road leading to the Sma' Glen. He watched the curlews as they flew backwards and forwards, their shrill cries breaking the fragile morning silence and on the hills beyond he thought he could see red deer grazing.

When he had left Glasgow soon after seven, Maggie had still been in her room, asleep and dreaming no doubt of the sentimental reconciliation with Simon to come, so he had started his journey on no more than a cup of coffee and was ready for the excellent breakfast which the inn provided. He had chosen the Foulford Inn partly because it was convenient for the first call he wished to make, but also because Mrs Hastie had mentioned, when he had spoken with her the previous afternoon, that Iain MacNair had frequently stopped there on his journeys to the north, either to take the breakfast after an early start or dropping in for an evening meal on his way home. Evidently he had not been a man who had enjoyed cooking for himself.

When he had finished his porridge, Sanderson asked the girl who replaced the empty plate with one of eggs, bacon, sausages and tomato if she had known Iain MacNair. She replied that everyone at the inn and a good many of the regular customers had known him well. The news of his death had shocked them all for he had been friendly and well liked. Why, not long ago, he had taken his breakfast at the inn at the start of a journey north, just as Sanderson was doing. They had expected to see him that same evening on his way home, for he had said he would look in for supper, but he had never arrived. No one had thought much of it, supposing that he had been delayed or that his car might have broken down.

When he left the inn, instead of turning right towards the Sma'

Glen, Sanderson went the other way, turning off towards Monzie and circling the back of Crieft to reach Glenturret distillery, one of the smallest distilleries in Scotland. There he learned that Iain MacNair had paid a business call at the distillery on the day before he had disappeared, staying for half an hour and discussing the orders he wished to place for whisky with them the following season. No one at Glenturret could think of any reason why a man so friendly and kind as MacNair should have been murdered.

From Glenturret Sanderson drove back past the Foulford Inn and through the Sma' Glen, joining the main road to the north at Dunkeld. On so beautiful a morning he would have preferred to have taken a longer route, enjoying the wild splendour of the moors on the road to Aberfeldy and then making for Pitlochry, but conscious that he was due in Edinburgh by early evening, he decided he could not afford the luxury of a more beautiful but more leisurely drive.

On the A9, vastly improved since the last time he had used it, he drove to Aviemore in not much over the hour, cut off towards Grantown, crossed the Spey by the bridge on the road to Aberlour and pulled up at Tormore distillery soon afterwards. The manager at Tormore could not have been more helpful. Yes, Mr MacNair had called at the distillery on the date Sanderson mentioned but no, he had said nothing about going to Belfast and had neither telephoned his office at Cumbernauld nor asked anyone at Tormore to do so. He also offered Sanderson a dram which Sanderson, knowing he had more distilleries to visit and aware of the whisky trade's reputation for generous hospitality, prudently declined.

At Glenfarclas and Macallan the hospitality and the answers to his questions were the same. Iain MacNair had been known to both distilleries for many years and he had visited them both on the day before he had disappeared, but no one had heard talk of a journey to Belfast and no telephone calls had been made on his account. Sanderson declined the proffered whisky at Glenfarclas but succumbed to temptation at Macallan, telling himself that a man was at least entitled to one dram before his lunch.

He took his lunch a few miles up the road in the bar of the Rothes Glen Hotel, a mansion almost splendid enough to be called a castle, where, Mrs Hastie had told him, MacNair would usually stay on longer business trips to Speyside. It was at the Rothes Glen that Sanderson had his first piece of good fortune. One of the young girls who waited at table was observant as well as bonnie and not only recalled MacNair lunching there on his last visit, but looking out of the dining-room window had noticed him opening the hatchback of his Volvo, evidently to reassure himself that his rod, waders and other fishing tackle were all there. Sanderson also learned that MacNair and a group of his friends shared the fishing rights on a stretch of the Spey not far above Ballindalloch.

After leaving the Rothes Glen he drove back towards Craigellachie, turning off the main road before he reached the village and heading up over the moors to cross the Spey and rejoin the road to Grantown at Ballindalloch. The drive took him past a string of distilleries, many with Gaelic names that went back to the time when whisky was first made in Scotland more than a thousand years ago: Speyburn, Glen Grant, Caperdonich, Glenrothes, Macallan, Cardhu, Tamdhu and Knockando.

As he drove over the moors in the sunshine, Sanderson felt even more strongly the nostalgia for his childhood which had assailed him almost as soon as his car had arrived at the foothills of the Highlands that morning. It was true that the gentle hills and wooded glens around the Spey were very different from the wild and savage beauty of the Western Highlands where he had lived as a boy, but the air had the same invigorating freshness, the landscape the same distant silence and the same colours. He had almost forgotten the colours that the north of Scotland had to offer; the greens of grass and trees and the purples of heather which in bright sunshine could be unnaturally bright and luminous, merging in the distance with the blue of hill and mountain and the blue itself changing suddenly to a whole range of deep purples and indigoes and in the evenings a deep blue-black. Sanderson realized now that he had been away from the real Scotland too long.

Glen Cromach distillery had been built on a hill not far from the valley through which ran the Livet, the most famous burn in Scotland, but it drew its water from another burn which ran through the peat moss on the hill and tumbled down in a cascade by the side of the distillery. Half a dozen cottages in which the workers lived were clustered around the distillery buildings and the manager had a slightly larger but still unpretentious house close enough for him to be easily roused should he be needed at any hour of day or night. A mile away and partly hidden in a copse of larch trees was the white farmhouse of the distillery owner, Major Hamish Stewart.

Stewart was in the distillery office when Sanderson arrived. He was a short, cheerful man dressed in a heavy tweed suit, a checked shirt that was frayed at the collar and cuffs and a Glenalmond tie. A fine salmon, all of 30 lbs, was mounted in a glass case on the wall behind his desk, two fishing rods and a pair of waders had been stowed carelessly in a corner of the office and a selection of brightly coloured salmon flies lay in the pen tray of the desk.

When he learned the reason for Sanderson's visit he exclaimed, 'Shocking business! I read about it in the papers. Poor Iain. He was a good egg.'

'Had you known him long?'

'Ever since I came to Speyside. He has had a rod on the Spey for years.'

'And you did business with him as well?'

'Yes, but that was more recent. Not long ago he told me that he had decided to use our whisky in one of the blends which his company put up and that he would be ordering fillings from us regularly from now on. It was good news, I can tell you.'

Sanderson seemed to detect a nuance behind the remark, the reluctant optimism of a man who had known hard times and was slow to accept that they might be over. He was curious enough to ask a question which might be resented coming from a stranger. 'Why? Has business been bad?'

'Not disastrously so, but we can always do with more orders. Mind you, I'm not complaining. I knew that starting a distillery would be hard going.'

'Did you build Glen Cromach then?'

Stewart told him that a distillery had originally been built in Glen Cromach in the middle of the last century but, like many others, it had been forced out of business during the slump in the whisky trade which followed the spectacular collapse of the Leith firm of Pattisons in 1898. The buildings had stood ruined and idle for more than 60 years until

Stewart had left the army with an unshakeable ambition to own a distillery. Somehow he had raised enough capital from his family, his friends and his bank to rebuilt Glen Cromach.

'Starting a distillery is not so much a gamble as an act of faith,' Stewart said. 'Until you start distilling you really don't know how the whisky is going to turn out. Of course there had been a distillery here before and as far as I could make out from old records and books on the trade, it had made a decent enough dram. But tastes in whisky have changed. It was only when I had invested tens of thousands in pot stills and mash tuns and washbacks that I could produce a sample of our make to show to the blenders and try to persuade them that Glen Cromach was good enough to put in their blends.'

'What makes the difference between a good whisky and an indifferent one?'

'The water mostly, and skill, of course. If you have the right water supply you should be able to make an acceptable dram.'

'Glen Cromach must be all right if Iain MacNair chose it,' Sanderson said, feeling he should be polite.

'That's true, but it was pure chance that made him decide to fill with us. It seems he was checking his company's inventories of whisky one day and discovered they owned a few hogsheads of Glen Cromach which Peter Wandercliff had filled back in his broking days. Iain asked us to send him a sample. Soon afterwards we filled a hogshead of new whisky for him and when he was next up here he ordered some more and told me he would be filling with us regularly in future.'

Sanderson remembered the letter from the manager of Glen Cromach which he had seen in the filing cabinet at MacNair's home. He asked Stewart, 'Didn't you deliver a cask of new whisky to Cumbernauld earlier this year?'

'Yes. And one of the twelve-year-old which we were keeping here for his company.'

'Is it not unusual to take new whisky away from the distillery warehouse?'

'Unusual but not unknown. Some of the larger blending firms have warehouses of their own in the south. Iain must have had his reasons.'

Sanderson decided that there was nothing to be gained from telling Stewart about MacNair's attempts to make a drinkable whisky without

87

maturing it. The story would take too long in the telling and now that MacNair was dead he had no wish to paint him as an eccentric, which was how most people in the whisky business would regard a man who had embarked on such an unrewarding crusade. So he asked another question instead.

'What exactly is the function of a whisky broker?'

'A broker provides a service for the industry.'

All the major whisky companies, Stewart went on to explain, held stocks of the different whiskies which they used in their blends. They would order the quantities of whisky which they estimated they would require from the distilleries concerned, who would fill the whisky into casks provided by the customer and keep it in their warehouses until the blender sent for it. Since the new whisky would not be used for several years, the whisky companies had to forecast what the sales of their brands would be in anywhere between four to fifteen years ahead and order enough whisky to cover that forecast. Inevitably the forecasts did not always prove to be accurate, with the result that a company would find itself short of one or more of the whiskies when the time came to blend, bottle and market their brands. In these cases they would use the services of a broker who would purchase the whisky for them from other companies who held stocks surplus to their needs.

'A good broker knows where he can lay his hands on the whisky his customer wants,' Stewart concluded.

'So he buys it and has it shipped to the firm who wants it?'

'Nothing so complicated as that. Once he has been paid the owner of the whisky will simply make out a delivery order to the bonded warehouse where the whisky is being held, usually a distillery warehouse.'

'And what exactly is a delivery order?'

'A very simple document.' Stewart smiled. 'We like to keep the paperwork in our industry down to the very minimum. In effect the delivery order informs the warehouse keeper that the whisky is now the property of the purchaser. The warehouse keeper amends his register accordingly and keeps the whisky where it is until the new owner sends for it.'

'Broking must be a very profitable business,' Sanderson remarked. 'I was told that Peter Wandercliff made a million out of broking before he set up his blending company.'

88

'Somebody is having you on!' Stewart laughed. 'He didn't make much out of the business he did in our whisky, I can tell you. He bought a few casks years ago, on spec I believe, but then seemed to lose interest in us. And as I've already told you very few of the big firms used Glen Cromach in their blends at that time.'

'How long is it since you last saw Iain MacNair?' Sanderson asked him.

Stewart scratched at his temple with a fingernail as he tried to work out the answer. 'Two months at least, more likely three. We were expecting he would call a week or two back but he didn't turn up.'

'Have you any idea why?'

'No, unless the fishing was too good that afternoon.'

'Did he always fish when he came up to Speyside?'

'Almost always. Combining business with pleasure, he called it. He would make as many of his calls as he could in the morning, even if it meant his leaving home at first light, then have a quick lunch and get down on the water for two or three hours. If he was due to call here, he would leave us till last as we are on his way home and because he knew he could always come and see me in my home if the distillery office was closed.'

'But the last time he didn't arrive at all?'

'No. We never saw him.'

'Do you know whereabouts on the river he fished?' Sanderson asked.

'Surely. I'll show you.'

After rummaging in a cupboard in a corner of the office, Stewart pulled out a framed, hand-drawn map showing the reaches of the Spey between Grantown and Craigellachie. At one time it must have hung on the office wall, but the picture wire which had supported it had snapped and no one had found the energy to repair it. Placing the map on his desk, Stewart pointed out to Sanderson the stretch of river where MacNair and a group of his friends had rented the fishing rights.

'I saw him fishing there more than once.' Stewart placed one finger on the map at a shallow bend in the river. 'Just here. He would park his car just off the road that runs along the north bank.'

'I think I'll go and take a look at the spot.'

Stewart looked at him but was too well-mannered to ask why anyone

89

should wish to look at the place where a dead man once fished. He said, 'Well, if you come back this way and you're druthy, look in for a dram. My wife would like to meet you.'

'Thanks but I doubt I'll have the time. I have a dinner date in Edinburgh this evening.'

Stewart came out of the office with him and walked him to his car. Just as he was about to start the engine Sanderson remembered another matter which he had intended to mention. 'By the way, I read in the papers that your former distillery manager died in Portugal a short time ago.'

'Fraser? Yes, poor chap. He retired early when he inherited money unexpectedly and went to live in Portugal. Then his wife died and now he's gone. Ironic, isn't it, how often life kicks a man in the teeth just as he thinks he's got everything he ever wanted?'

'The papers suggested he might have died from gas poisoning. Do you suppose it might have been suicide?'

'Fraser? No way! He had no pity for himself nor for anyone else. He was as tough as old boots.'

Leaving the distillery Sanderson drove back to cross the Spey below Ballindalloch and then turned left along the road to Grantown, a much narrower but much more attractive route than the main road on the opposite side. He found the spot which Stewart had shown him on the map without difficulty. Another man was fishing the same stretch, standing up to his thighs in the river and casting his line out over the water with easy dexterity. The man's Ford was parked in the same place where, no doubt, MacNair had been accustomed to leave his Volvo, in a small clearing on the other side of the road from the river. The land beyond the clearing was thickly wooded and the trees deep in bracken. Anyone who wished to lie in wait for the man who was fishing could easily have concealed himself among the trees only a few feet from where the Ford stood and jumped him when he came back from the river and was taking off his waders.

## 11

THAT MORNING SIR Douglass Tweedie had been watching critically as his foursomes partner, a young man named MacKenzie from the bank's Perth branch, took out an iron to play his shot to the eighteenth green at Muirfield. They had seen a lead of three holes slip away and now stood all square playing the last hole, with their opponents' ball lying indecently close to the green in two.

'Don't be short,' Sir Douglass said severely.

He knew that young men, even those with a handicap of three at Carnoustie, were not to be trusted on the golf course. In his experience they all believed they could hit the ball further than they actually could. Forgetting that it was his failure to get out of a bunker at the thirteenth hole, his shank with a wedge at the sixteenth and his nasty little twitch of a simple putt at the seventeenth which had been responsible for squandering their lead, he had convinced himself that MacKenzie was letting him down. Even the miserable little squirt of 50 yards or so with which he had followed MacKenzie's majestic drive at the eighteenth had not shaken this belief and he had already made a mental resolve to send the bank's inspectors to the Perth branch at an early date.

Sir Douglass hated losing at golf. Quite apart from the financial loss — he had allowed himself to be persuaded to wager a whole pound on this game — it irritated him to accept that other men, often men of no consequence in business, could play golf better than he did.

When MacKenzie finally played, a beautiful soaring shot which curled into the green and settled no more than fifteen feet short of the hole, he said ungraciously, 'You'd have done better to take one more club.'

They walked with their opponents towards the green. Normally

91

Sir Douglass only played golf at weekends and while on holiday, for he believed that mid-week golf was a frivolous luxury which interfered with the serious business of making money. He made one exception and that was the annual match between teams from Scottish and International Distillers and their bankers, the Strathclyde Linen Bank. At one time the match had been played over 36 holes but now, to take account of the increasing ages of the senior members of both teams, they played one round of foursomes in the morning, followed by a gargantuan and bucolic lunch and only a few of the younger players went out to play a few more holes in the afternoon.

Sir Douglass and MacKenzie were playing in the top match against George Wishart, the chairman of Scottish and International Distillers, who had also chosen a young partner, a Scottish internationalist named Morrison. Wishart, himself a low handicap golfer, now had to play his side's shot to the green from no more than 30 yards and surprisingly he fluffed it, leaving their ball just short of the putting surface.

This unexpected bonus cheered Sir Douglass, for there was now every prospect of the hole and the match being halved and one pound being saved. Picking up his side's ball he marked its position, not using either a marker or a coin, but by scratching a line on the grass with the point of a tee-peg. In a friendly match no one was likely to object to this technical breach of the rules. Morrison then chipped up from the edge of the green but struck the shot too firmly and left it some four feet beyond the hole.

'Your putt, Douglass,' Wishart said. 'I hope you won't be so unfriendly as to hole it.'

Sir Douglass went forward, bent down as though looking for the scratch he had made in the green and then confidently placed his ball a good eighteen inches nearer the hole than it had been when he had picked it up. He was sure that none of the other players in the match would have noticed this little deception, just as they had seemed to be unaware of the two occasions earlier in the round when he had improved the lie of his ball in the rough by surreptitiously nudging it with his foot. Sadly, however, all the men with whom he was playing that day, and a good many others, knew that Sir Douglass was a cheat, but they chose to ignore the fact. Now, having replaced the ball, he putted and left it rather more than a yard short of the hole.

'That's good enough Douglass,' Wishart said at once, knocking the ball away. 'Stone dead! A fine putt!'

His own ball lay only an inch or two further from the hole than Sir Douglass's had, but not waiting to see if the putt would be conceded, he bent down over it. Struck firmly but with an open blade of the putter, the ball missed the right-hand side of the hole with some comfort. As they all shook hands and headed for the clubhouse, Sir Douglass was the only one of the four who did not appreciate how skilfully Wishart and his partner had contrived to lose the match.

Back in the clubhouse after four rounds of drinks they lunched on chicken soup, steak and kidney pie, treacle tart and cheese. Then MacKenzie and Morrison went out to play another nine holes, leaving Sir Douglass and Wishart to drink their coffee and liqueurs alone.

'Dreadful business about poor Iain MacNair!' Wishart remarked.

'Dreadful!'

'Still I suppose he was mixing with some pretty odd characters after he parted company with the brewers.'

'Precisely.'

Wishart took their glasses over to the table where the liqueurs stood ready and poured two more kummels. 'One doesn't like to be uncharitable,' he observed, 'but at least now we'll be spared that crusade of Iain's about maturation. Some of the smaller companies in the industry were beginning to think there was something to be said for his idea.'

'Of course they would!' Sir Douglass said contemptuously. 'That's pure self-interest. They don't have money tied up in stocks.'

'He might have ended up by dividing the industry.'

'As you know I was never too concerned about his campaign to have the Finance Act amended. That was a non-starter. But he told me that he had another scheme which would have caused us all problems, and I believed him.'

'Did he say what it was?'

'No. You know how secretive he had become.'

'Well we won't have to worry about that now.'

93

'Don't be too sure. Self-congratulations may be premature.'

'What makes you say that?'

'Iain's girl, Katriona, has set some young man to work looking into her father's death. He came to see me yesterday. A bright chap. Too bright. God knows what he'll find out about Iain's plans if he keeps on nosing around.'

'Surely,' Wishart said, 'there must be a way of stopping him.'

Katriona and Sanderson dined in the smaller of the two dining-rooms at Prestonfield House, a sixteenth century building designed by the architect of Holyrood House and one where the peacocks on the lawns seemed in no way out of place. Katriona was wearing a dark-blue dress, very little make-up and no jewellery of any kind. In the setting of the dining-room, with its ornate painted ceiling, the many fine pictures on its walls and its gleaming antique furniture, she looked almost drab, without colour and without vitality.

On the drive from her flat she had scarcely spoken. Sanderson did not mind for her silence did not make him feel uncomfortable. Some women he knew used silence as a weapon of disapproval, others felt obliged to fill it with idle chatter, but Katriona, he sensed, valued silence and used it naturally and without affectation.

Even after they had ordered their meal, she did not mention her reason for suggesting that they should meet that evening. Sanderson was glad, for there would be time enough to talk about her father's death later. He had the feeling that if he could get to know and understand Katriona, their relationship might become less formal and therefore easier. Now that he had become immersed in the circumstances surrounding Iain MacNair's murder, he no longer felt as though he was working for her and had already resolved that he would take no payment for what he had so far done and might do in the future.

So he talked of other things, gradually drawing Katriona into conversation. Sensing that she might resent questions about her own life, he spoke instead of his, of his parents who had been born on Skye and then gone to farm in Ardnamurchan, that peninsula of land just north of the island of Mull that stretched out into the Atlantic, ending in the most westerly point of Britain's mainland. He talked about

Ardnamurchan and the coastline to the north of it, with its broad sea lochs and countless small islands; about the farms and the crofts, the narrow winding roads and the ferries, on which a ten-minute crossing of a sea loch could save two hours of motoring. He talked of the dignity and independence of the Highlanders and recounted stories of the characters he had known, wonderful eccentrics in their own way, but winning more affection than mockery.

'Do you know the Highlands?' he asked Katriona.

'I've only once been north of Pitlochry.'

'When was that?'

'My father once took me camping in Wester Ross when I was about six. I loved it but came home covered in cuts and bruises and midge bites and my mother, who had been totally against the idea anyway, never let me go again.' The memory seemed to amuse her and she laughed.

'You did not have a brother?'

'No. My mother is a vain and self-centred woman. I've always known that. I suppose she decided that child-bearing was a painful, messy business which interfered with her social life and decided not to embark on it again.'

Sanderson almost remarked that Brenda MacNair had done pretty well with the one child she had produced, but he thought better of it. Paying facile compliments to women was a habit he had allowed himself to acquire in London but one which was not so highly valued in Scotland, where sincerity and plain speaking were still considered virtues. Besides, he had the impression that Katriona was at last beginning to relax and lose a little of her stiffness. That may have been the Château Talbot they were drinking but he was vain enough to believe she was also enjoying his company and did not wish to risk damaging this fragile entente with what she might see as empty flattery.

It was not until they had finished dinner and moved to one of the drawing-rooms on the first floor to take coffee, that she raised the subject of her father's death.

'Did you find out anything on Speyside?'

'I believe I know exactly how your father was killed.' Sanderson paused and looked at her. 'Would you prefer not to talk about it?'

'No. I want to know.'

'I have traced your father's movements on the day before he disappeared up until the middle of the afternoon. He drove north that day, stopping for breakfast just beyond Crief and visiting one distillery there. Later in the morning he called at three other distilleries on Speyside and lunched at a hotel in Rothes Glen.'

'And then?'

He told Katriona that after lunch MacNair had evidently gone to fish the Spey, that he had never kept his appointment at Glen Cromach distillery nor stopped for an evening meal at the Foulford Inn. Mrs Duncan was convinced that he had never spent that night at his home in Bridge of Allan, all of which led to only one possible conclusion. He had been attacked and probably murdered either while he was fishing or immediately afterwards when he was preparing to leave the river.

'Whoever killed your father must have used his Volvo to bring him south.' Sanderson found himself choosing his phrases carefully, trying to avoid pejorative words like 'murder' and 'body'. At the same time he wondered why he did so, for Katriona showed no signs of flinching from the reality of truth.

'And they drove his body over to Northern Ireland on the ferry the next day,' she suggested, 'and then dropped it into the sea.'

'I wouldn't think so. The Volvo might have been searched as it entered Ireland. No. I imagine they — and there may well have been more than one person involved — drove down from Speyside during the night and hid your father somewhere in Dumfriesshire. The next day one of them took the Volvo on the ferry to Larne and abandoned it outside Belfast, returning either as a passenger on the ferry or by air to Glasgow. Then when it suited them they must have taken your father out to sea in a boat, at night no doubt. They might have hoped that his body would never reappear and if it did people would assume that he had been murdered in Northern Ireland.'

In the warmth and luxury of the drawing-room of Prestonfield House, surrounded by bright chatter and laughter, violent death seemed far enough away to be unreal. Sanderson felt schizoid, as though only one of his two personae were in the room while the other was witnessing the events he was describing, watching MacNair's dead body float face up a fathom below the surface of a dark sea.

'You don't know who killed my father?' Katriona's question interrupted his fantasy.

'No one with whom he associated would be able to plan a cold-blooded murder and execute it so efficiently.'

'One could find men to do it for money.'

'At one time they were ten a penny in Glasgow. I imagine there are still a few left,' he agreed.

Katriona nodded. Although she would be too young to remember the days when Glasgow was a centre of organized crime and vice, ruled by warring gangs, she must have heard or read about them.

'Who would want my father dead badly enough to pay someone to kill him?' she asked.

'He appears to have upset a number of people in his line of business.'

'And would they have gone to such lengths to get rid of him?'

Sanderson shrugged his shoulders. 'Money is always a powerful motive and we're talking about hundreds of millions of pounds.'

'Talking of money, did you know that my father was a wealthy man?' Katriona asked, and Sanderson realized that her question was not as casual as it sounded.

'Had he inherited money?'

'His father left him comfortably off but he came into a great deal of money more recently than that. When my grandfather sold the family business he did a very shrewd deal. He took only as much of the purchase price in cash as he needed to pay the death duties we owed and to buy himself an annuity. The rest of it was in the form of North British Brewery shares for my father, with the proviso that when my father died or if he left the company the brewery would buy them back from him at the current price quoted on the Stock Exchange. At the time of the sale North British was really quite a modest concern, but since then it has grown into a multinational conglomerate, with pubs and wine and spirit companies and even hotels throughout Britain and Europe. The shares are worth many times more than they were when my father acquired them and when he left North British he sold them for a fortune.'

'How do you know all this, Sanderson asked, 'if you haven't seen him for years?'

97

'That is what I wanted to tell you tonight. Not long ago — it was probably when you and my father were tramping the Highlands — my mother came to see me. She came to my office, which was as it should be.' Katriona's voice hardened with bitterness. 'For she was wanting free legal advice, that's all.'

'You're surely not going to tell me she wanted to get her hands on your father's money?'

'Only a man would be cynical enough to have guessed the truth. Yes, that's exactly what my mother wanted. She asked me, if you please, whether there was any legal way by which she could force my father to give her any of the money.'

'But that's absurd! She has remarried.'

'You'll be even more astounded by her effrontery when you hear the whole story. When she came to see me it all came out. For the first time I learnt the truth about my parent's separation and divorce. I learnt the truth about my mother.'

Her parents had separated, Katriona said, while she was in her last year at boarding school. She had returned home for the school holidays to find that her father had left her mother and, although no explicit reason was given, she was led to believe that he had gone to live with another woman. Then Jock Ferguson, whom she had always thought of as a family friend, began to visit the house more frequently and sometimes he stayed for the night. Less than a year later he had moved in permanently and he and her mother had married.

Katriona had never liked Ferguson very much, but she had been impressed with the attention which he had paid to her mother and to herself. His only concern had seemed to be to give them both a good time. He had taken them everywhere, to the best restaurants, to the races at Ayr, on weekends in London when they all three stayed at the Savoy, gambled at exclusive clubs, danced at discothèques which were supposed to be frequented by royalty.

'At eighteen,' she concluded, 'I was naîve enough to believe he was being kind, trying to make up to my mother for the humiliation of having her husband walk out on her.'

'And now you know that wasn't so?'

'When my mother came to see me about the money, I suddenly guessed the truth. I asked her straight out and she admitted that she and Jock had been lovers for months before my father left home. He left to make things easier for them, to make room for that vulgar little bastard.'

It was an evening for first times, Sanderson decided. Katriona had laughed for the first time since he had met her, expressed not disdain but genuine anger for the first time, sworn for the first time. He wondered whether she had any more surprises in store for him.

'When their marriage broke up,' Katriona said, 'my father gave my mother what was by any standards a generous settlement and allowed her to stay on in the family home. What's more, after she remarried, he not only paid for my university course but gave us both an allowance. A dress allowance he called it but it was a good deal more than pin money, I can tell you.'

'And she wanted more?'

'By some twisted piece of logic she has convinced herself that it is her right. She maintains that if he had come into all that money before they were divorced he would have been obliged to settle at least one third of it on her. When I assured her that she had no legal right to it and told her I thought her behaviour was despicable, she stormed out of my office in a rage. I haven't seen or spoken to her since.'

'Was that why you wrote to your father?'

'Yes. I realized how shamefully I'd treated him and wanted to make amends.'

She poured herself another cup of coffee from the pot, even though by that time it must have been cold, put in a spoonful of sugar and stirred it impatiently. One could not tell whether her irritation was caused by indignation at her mother's behaviour or a feeling of guilt for the way she herself had treated her father. When they had left Prestonfield House and were driving back to her flat, she scarcely spoke, but when he drew the Mercedes to a halt outside the building she looked at him, hesitating it seemed.

Then she said abruptly, 'Would you like to come up and have a drink or a coffee?'

'A coffee would be great.'

She left him in the drawing-room while she went to make the coffee, for Gillian who, he had learned earlier, was at a concert in the Usher Hall, had not yet returned. While he was waiting he looked around the room. It was curiously lacking in both femininity and personality, a room shared by two bachelor girls who had not cared enough to make it a home. Sanderson was struck by its resemblance to the dull, anonymous drawing-room in MacNair's house at Bridge of Allan.

When Katriona returned, she handed him his cup of coffee and then sat next to him on the sofa. Looking at her as she came into the room, he wondered whether she had touched up her make-up, for there appeared to be more colour in her face, an effect of eye-shadow perhaps. He could not be sure, but when she sat down next to him, he realized at once that while she had been out of the room she had put on perfume; not an expensive perfume like other women he knew would wear, Dior or Nina Ricci or Worth, but something rather unsubtle and cloying, a perfume which a girl with little interest in fashion might choose. Had she been wearing perfume earlier in the evening, he would certainly have noticed it when they were in the car together.

'What will happen to your father's money now?' he asked her.

'I've no idea. We'll be hearing from his solicitors soon I imagine,' she replied and then, with a little spurt of anger, she added, 'In view of the way she treated him, I only hope he hasn't left anything to my mother. I'd rather he left it to a cats' home.'

'Did she try asking him for money before she came to see you?'

'Oh yes. She wanted a hundred thousand pounds.'

'Do you know when she asked him?'

'At a dinner party shortly before.'

'Dinner at her house? That must have been the night he was almost killed driving home.'

'At his house, you mean,' Katriona said sourly. 'Yes. I know about the dinner party. I was invited too.'

'But you didn't go?'

'No. At that time I had no wish to meet my father for I didn't know what I know now. In retrospect I'm glad I declined the invitation for I know what my mother had in mind. The dinner was a little ploy to bring me and my father together, effect a reconciliation. She calculated he'd be so delighted that in a mood of euphoria he'd agree to give her the hundred thousand. And I think he might have done. But

100

he refused and it was then that she came to me for free legal advice.'

The bitterness in her words and in her expression were less than one might have expected. Was it because her disillusionment at her mother's behaviour and her regret for the way she had treated her father were also more painful than she had suggested, Sanderson wondered. He wondered too whether other disappointments in the past had immunized her against deep emotion.

'Is your mother badly off? From what you said earlier her second husband must have money.'

'He did have, and spent it freely. That's what attracted my mother to him. But now I suspect that his business must be doing badly.'

'What is his business?'

'Can't you guess? He's a bookmaker.'

When Sanderson had finished his coffee and was leaving, Katriona insisted on coming downstairs with him. As they stood in the front doorway she said, 'Let me know what you find out, won't you?'

'Are you sure you wish me to continue with these enquiries?'

'Quite sure, provided you don't object.'

'I don't object. But I don't promise that I'll achieve anything.'

She stood in the open doorway and watched as he got into his Mercedes and drove away but she did not wave. The streets of Edinburgh were almost empty, so he made the motorway in not much more than ten minutes and was dropping down off the flyover into the centre of Glasgow not long afterwards. Luck was with him for a change, and he found a place to park in the street within about a hundred yards of Maggie's flat. When he reached the entrance to the building and was pulling out his key to open the door, he was stopped by a policeman who was standing nearby.

'Excuse me sir, may I ask if you stay here?'

'I do.'

'What flat would that be, sir?'

'Number four, on the second floor.'

'Then would you be Mr Sanderson?' the policeman asked, and when Sanderson nodded he said, 'Then you may go up, sir.'

'What is this? What's happened?'

'Inspector Crawford will tell you about it. He's with the young woman now.'

A second policeman was stationed on the stairs between the first and second floors and his role was evidently to prevent anyone walking on a section of the stairs close to the bannisters. He allowed Sanderson to pass on the other side, telling him to keep as close to the wall as possible. Sanderson did not waste time asking him any questions.

He found Maggie in the flat, sitting in an armchair facing a burly man who had drawn up a hard-backed chair opposite hers. Another policeman in plain clothes was standing listening to their conversation. When Sanderson went into the room, Maggie got quickly to her feet and came towards him. Her face was white and he could see fear in her eyes.

'Simon's dead,' she said simply.

## 12

MAGGIE'S STORY WAS that Simon had promised that he would arrive for what she planned as their *dîner à deux* by seven-thirty at the latest. When eight o'clock came and he still had not put in an appearance she was not particularly worried. Simon was neither very punctual nor very good at sticking to the letter of his promises. Soon after eight she had thought she had heard a noise coming from the stairs which led to her flat but had taken no notice of it. There were two small flats on the third storey of the building, both occupied by young men who not infrequently made a good deal of noise as they stumbled up the stairs at night.

At about eight-thirty, for no reason that she could explain, she had opened the front door of her flat and looked out. The staircase was in darkness, for the lights were operated by switches on each landing which automatically switched them off again after a few seconds. When she pressed the switch outside her door she saw Simon lying on the stairs halfway between the first and second floors.

'I was furious,' she told Sanderson. 'You see, I thought he was drunk and had passed out. But he was dead.'

Much had happened since then. Maggie had telephoned for an ambulance and when the ambulance men realized that Simon was dead, they had sent for the police. Eventually Simon's body had been taken away and when the police searched the stairs they had found the top half of a broken bottle on the first-floor landing and what was left of the remainder in shattered fragments all over the stairs. Simon did not appear to have been cut by the glass, however, and the only wound the police surgeon had been able to find on him was a severe bruise above his left temple. A further examination would be needed to determine whether the bruise had been made by the bottle. The police had questioned the occupants of all the other flats in the building, but no one admitted to seeing or hearing any intruder or an attack or even the sounds of a struggle. For almost two hours the police had been questioning Maggie and now Inspector Crawford turned his attention to Sanderson.

'You are staying in this flat are you not, sir?'

'Yes, for the time being.'

'So it is not your permanent address?'

'No. I only recently moved to Glasgow from London.'

'And do you intend to stay on in Glasgow?'

'I've not decided on my plans as yet.' Sanderson could see no reason for telling the police that where he would settle permanently would depend on where he found employment.

'How well did you know the deceased?'

'Not very well. We only met when I moved to Glasgow.'

'Was he staying here as well?'

Sanderson may have been over-sensitive in feeling that Crawford's question implied a hint of disapproval, a Presbyterian disapproval of what he may have suspected was some kind of immoral *ménage à trois*. He replied, 'As I'm sure you have already been told by Miss Semple, he spent the night here from time to time.'

'Can you think of any reason why the deceased should have been assaulted?'

'Assaulted? Murdered, you mean? No, no reason at all.'

'Would you mind telling me where you have been this evening?'

'I was having dinner in Edinburgh.'

'And at what time did you leave Edinburgh?'

'Less than an hour ago.'

'Is there anyone who can confirm that, sir?'

'The young lady with whom I had dinner would, I'm sure. Shall I give you her address and telephone number?' Sanderson spread sarcasm on the question like a heavy-handed bricklayer splashing on cement.

'Not now,' Crawford replied, and then to cut the cheeky young sod down to size he added, 'but I'll take it from you before we leave.'

After several more questions, none of them of much consequence, Crawford appeared to decide that he had done enough for the night. He thought of taking both Maggie and Sanderson to C.I.D. headquarters for further questioning, but apathy or boredom or fatigue were stronger than temptation. He had already made up his mind that there was nothing spectacular about this killing and sensed that it would not be worth more than a couple of paragraphs in the newspapers of a city where crime was commonplace. There would not be enough kudos for him in solving it to lose a night's sleep and next day, no doubt, after a little more intensive questioning, it would solve itself.

Before he left he said, 'You'll not be leaving Glasgow, madam, sir, without telling me? We'll be needing to talk to you again and to take your statements.'

'No,' they replied in unison.

'I'm for away then. But there'll be a man on duty outside all night.'

Maggie watched him leave with his sergeant and did not speak until they were both out of the flat and she had heard the front door shut. Then she said, 'Bruce, he thinks I killed Simon.'

'Don't be absurd!'

'He does. You didn't hear the questions he asked me; question after question, all of them revolving around the same point, never asking me outright whether I had killed Simon but trying to trick me into admitting that I had.'

'You're imagining it.' Even as he made the comment Sanderson remembered Maggie's outburst of fury at Simon a few evenings previously; the ashtray she had hurled at him, her remark that one day she would kill the sod. He put the thought out of his mind. He would never believe that Maggie could be really violent.

'Look at things from the point of view of the police. Whoever killed Simon attacked him as he was climbing the stairs on his way here. That leaves two possibilities. They could have been lying in wait for him, but in that case how did they get into the building? The door to the street is always kept locked at night and one needs a key to get in. The second possibility is that I was waiting for Simon, in a rage because he was late, and when I heard him arrive I went out and hit him with a bottle as he came up the stairs.'

'Simon could have been followed into the house,' Sanderson said, and then, although it was not a charitable suggestion he added, 'he could have been followed here by some little ned whose girl friend he had been chatting up in a pub. You know Simon.'

'Then there's the bottle they found on the stairs.' Maggie ignored his attempts to reassure her. 'It was a malt whisky bottle, a twelve-year-old malt. Not the kind of bottle you would pick up in a sleazy pub or in the street if you were meaning to start a fight or cut someone up.'

'How could anyone as strong as Simon be killed by a bang on the head?'

'Do you suppose they'll arrest me tomorrow morning?'

'Of course not!'

'They don't allow bail on murder charges, do they? My God, that means I won't be able to do that TV show next Tuesday! Bruce, it's so important, that one! It could open up a whole new career for me.'

'Maggie, there's no question of your being charged with murder.'

'What you're saying is that it was only manslaughter. So you believe I killed him too!'

Sanderson looked at Maggie. Her face was still white and although she appeared to have her emotions under control, she was speaking rapidly, the words tumbling out after each other, sharp and disjointed. He sensed that she was balanced on the edge of hysteria. Crossing to the sideboard, he took out a bottle of whisky and two glasses.

'What are you doing?' she asked him suspiciously.

'You and I are going to have a drink and we're not going to talk any more about what happened.'

'Why not?'

'Because if we do we'll be up all night and that will solve nothing. There'll be plenty of time to talk, rationally and sensibly, in the morning.'

'Christ, you're a callous bastard!'

In spite of her protest, she did as he had suggested. As they drank the whisky, they talked of other things. Most of the conversation came from Sanderson. At first he tried reminiscing about their university days, but like most women of her age Maggie took little interest in the past, so he switched to talking about her work. Faced with a barrage of questions which she had no option but to answer, however grudgingly, she began to respond. They talked of the *Glasgow Chronicle* and of her colleagues on the paper, some of whom Sanderson had known as a student, of the difficulties which all newspapers were facing and of how they were adapting their style and presentation of the news to answer the competition of television.

Then they talked of television itself. Not long previously Maggie had interviewed an ageing American film actor, a man with a rugged, indestructible face and an equally rugged personality, who had been passing through Scotland on his way to make a film in Iceland. Sanderson had not watched the programme but Maggie had a video tape recording of it and now they watched it together. One had to admire the skill with which Maggie had handled the arrogant, self-centred old man, using not a persuasive charm but a very Scottish directness to draw out of him a succession of frank admissions, illustrated with amusing anecdotes.

The television and a second glass of whisky seemed to help her to relax and soon she was talking freely about her work. By then it was well past two o'clock and at the end of a long day Sanderson was finding difficulty in remaining awake. Maggie may have sensed this for suddenly she said, 'I'm ready for my bed.'

'Are you sure you'll sleep?'

'I'll take a pill.'

On her way out of the room she hesitated, looked at Sanderson and then came and kissed him lightly on the cheek. He assumed it was a token of gratitude for his patience and sympathy. After she had left he took the empty glasses into the kitchen, washed them, switched off the lights and went to his bedroom. A recurring picture kept troubling him, a mental picture of Simon coming up the stairs, unsteadily, for he would have taken a few drinks to fortify his resolution for the reconciliation with Maggie. Then whoever had been in wait for him had stepped out of the shadows to club him down. And having knocked him down his assailant would have smashed the bottle on the bannisters, ready to thrust the jagged edge into his face. But why? Revenge, no doubt, or simply malice, a desire to cut up the toffee-nosed bastard. But when he went to grab Simon and spoil his good looks, Simon was already dead.

The picture was still in Sanderson's mind when he fell asleep. He slept lightly, uneasily and it seemed for only a few minutes, waking when the door to his room opened.

Maggie's voice said plaintively, 'Bruce, I can't sleep.'

'Did you take a sleeping pill?'

'Yes.'

In the darkness he could not see her face, only the outline of her figure in a pale-coloured shortie nightdress. She looked forlorn, reminding him of a frightened child.

'Can I get in beside you?' she asked.

107

'Come Maggie, you're a big girl now; much too big to be getting into daddy's bed.'

She would not be put off by his flippancy but came and stood by the bed. He sensed rather than saw that she was shivering.

'Please, Bruce!'

'All right then.'

Maggie climbed into the bed and lay there, next to him but not touching him. He knew then that she was shivering and when he put his arm around her shoulders they felt icy cold although the night was warm. The protective gesture appeared to satisfy whatever need she had and she lay there without speaking. Presently her breathing grew deeper and he realized that she was asleep.

He slept too, or half slept, restlessly in a world of distorted faces and bizarre images. When consciousness returned he was aware of a sensation which he recognized only slowly as desire. Maggie had undone the single button of his pyjama trousers and her fingers were stroking his stomach.

'I don't think that's a very good idea,' he said, instantly awake and taking her hand he lifted it away.

'Yes! I want it! Yes!' She whispered urgently as her fingers reached out again.

'No, Maggie!'

Sitting up in the bed she tore her nightdress off and as she lifted her arms he could see her breasts, small but tempting. Her eyes seemed unnaturally bright, gleaming in the darkness.

'Bruce darling, don't reject me!' She pleaded with something like despair in her voice. 'Not tonight! Don't reject me!'

Without waiting for his reply, she swooped down on him, pressing her mouth against his and trying to prise open his lips with her tongue. Grabbing his hands she pressed them to her breasts. Even as he fought her, Sanderson recalled all the nights at university when he had lain alone wanting her, all the sexual fantasies that had tortured him. As he felt his willpower slipping he found himself thinking ironically that this must be the nearest a man could come to being raped.

When finally he gave in and began to respond to her urgency, Maggie began to cry. She made love ferociously, her caresses punctuated by sobs which grew progressively louder and more convulsive. Sanderson felt her tears drip on his face and noticed how warm they

108

were and how warm her breath was.

He knew that he was no more than a surrogate lover, a substitute for the dead Simon, but he did not mind, for the sensuality, the swift surge of physical excitement, was equal to anything he had imagined in those adolescent days.

When it was over, Maggie moved away and lay with her back towards him, still not speaking, her crying now no louder than a strangled whimper. He reached out and touched her shoulder gently, wishing to comfort her and felt her recoil. But the flinch was only momentary and then, ashamed of her instinctive reaction, she turned towards him and kissed his cheek.

'That was fantastic darling!' she said. 'The best ever!'

He knew she did not mean it but for a moment he loved her for the lie. In a minute or two the crying turned to sniffs, the sniffs stopped and she was asleep. This time Sanderson's mind was too active for sleep. The picture of Simon returned. Poor, inoffensive Simon, a hostage of his own restlessness, a prisoner of his good looks. Had whoever attacked him on the stairs even realized who his victim was? He may have surprised an intruder or more than one who had broken into the building and were prowling on the stairs, looking for a chance to rob one of the flats. Sanderson had heard of several other instances of that type of crime in both London and Glasgow. If the intruders had come later or if Simon had changed his mind and decided not to visit Maggie that night, it might have been Sanderson himself who had been clubbed down on the stairs.

Instantly that thought, itself no more than casual speculation, exploded into another which was frighteningly real. Whoever had murdered Iain MacNair would surely know by now of the enquiries that Sanderson had been making, of the journey he made to see the police at Stranraer, of his visits to MacNair's house at Bridge of Allan and to the distilleries on Speyside, perhaps even of the questions he had been asking. And what better way of discouraging an unhealthy curiosity than a slash with a broken bottle? And if that had been the intention, whoever had been waiting on the stairs would know it was the building where Sanderson lived but could not possibly have known that Simon would be visiting Maggie that evening.

'My God!' he thought. 'There can be no other explanation! Simon was mistaken for me!'

## 13

HAMISH GOUGH HAD come to believe that the position he held in the Scottish Development Agency could not have suited him better, even if he had written the job description himself. He liked the Agency's luxurious offices in a new building in Blythswood Street and he liked the people with whom he worked, an assortment of former civil servants, academics, economists, marketing men and journalists, most of them young and enthusiastic.

And most of all he enjoyed the work he had to do. He had no authority and took no decisions, which was as well for he had always flinched from decisions, but his colleagues asked for his advice, listened to it with at least a show of respect and not infrequently followed it. That, in Gough's opinion, was the proper function of a legally trained mind. In the two years he had spent with the Agency, he had come to love the place which he saw as a refuge from a wife who expected too much from him, children who treated him with amused indifference, unsympathetic friends and not least the bookmakers who were only too ready to exploit what he knew was his greatest weakness.

So when the police telephoned him at the Agency that morning he was immediately terrified in case his colleagues should hear of it. Any involvement with the police, even one which was long past and done with, might lose him his post. The S.D.A., although not technically a branch of the civil service, would, he supposed, expect the same irreproachable conduct and integrity from its staff.

When the chief inspector from the Glasgow C.I.D. 'phoned to say that the police wished to speak to Gough and offered to send a car to fetch him from his office, he declined at once. He did not even ask why the police wished to see him. Instead he invented an excuse for leaving the office and walked round to C.I.D. headquarters, hurrying as though by speed alone he might be able to force a lid down on whatever unsavoury smells might leak out of the police's enquiries.

Chief Inspector Forbes had a round, innocent face and a smile which he was not afraid to use, but the Glasgow underworld knew him as a hard man. Gough knew that and so was at an immediate disadvantage in the game they were about to play.

'You'll know why I asked you to come round here today of course, Mr Gough,' Forbes opened.

'I have no idea; not the slightest,' Gough lied.

'Then you'll not have heard that Mr Iain MacNair has been murdered?'

Gough hesitated before he replied with another lie, but only for an instant. 'No.'

'His body was washed up out of the sea near Stranraer. But he had been killed beforehand, you'll understand.'

'I didn't know.'

'Had you seen anything of Mr MacNair these past few weeks?'

'You're not accusing me of murdering him! Man, that's ridiculous!' The slow, insidious panic that was creeping up on him drove Gough to blustering.

'No one is accusing you of anything, sir. We're just asking you a few questions.'

'But why, man?'

'Come, sir.' Forbes's voice hardened. 'You'll not be expecting us to have forgotten that business of the letters, surely?'

'That was a long time ago.'

Privately, Forbes did not believe for a moment that Gough had been responsible for Iain MacNair's death. The threatening letters which MacNair had brought to the police had been laughably easy to trace. A few simple enquiries had established that Gough had been dismissed from the legal department of the North British Brewery for his negligence in negotiating the agreement between the company and MacNair when the latter had resigned. Gough had typed the threatening letters on a battered old portable which he kept at home and posted them in a pillar-box not a hundred yards from his front door.

'And as you know, Inspector, MacNair didn't press charges

111

against me for those letters. So why should I murder him?'

'You haven't answered my question, sir. Had you seen Mr MacNair in recent weeks?' Although he was certain Gough would not have had the cunning or the bottle needed for what had been a well-planned murder, Forbes had not ruled out the possibility that he might in some way be involved.

'What are you suggesting, Inspector? That I killed him in Glasgow or at his home in Bridge of Allan? How would I have got his body down to Dumfriesshire? As you know I don't possess a car.'

'Did you not say you had not heard that Mr MacNair was dead?'

'Yes.'

'Then how did you know where his body was found?'

A rising panic clutched at Gough's throat, preventing him from making any reply. Could one be arrested and charged simply for lying to the police? His speciality had been company law and he had forgotten the little he had learned about criminal law. He wondered whether he would be suspended immediately when the head of the Agency heard of his arrest and dismissed later. Was that not how civil servants were treated?

'Had you seen Mr MacNair at all recently?' Forbes asked.

'Not to speak to. I saw him once in the street, just by chance you'll understand.'

'When was that?'

'A wee while back. About three weeks ago maybe, but I cannot be sure.'

'And you say you didn't speak with him?'

'No. I doubt he even noticed me.'

'Where was this?'

'I was passing the entrance to the Midas Club as MacNair came out. He was with another man,' Gough replied and then, hoping that it might help his own case, he added, 'They seemed to be quarrelling.'

'Did you know the other man?'

'No, Inspector.'

Forbes sighed inwardly. Why was it, he wondered, that as soon as they faced the police, some folk, even decent, honest, trustworthy folk, could not help lying.

*  *  *

112

At the same time as Forbes was interviewing Gough, his subordinate, Detective-Inspector Crawford, was questioning Miss Margaret Semple, the young woman outside whose door a man had been found dead the previous evening. Miss Semple was as nervous as Gough was, but Crawford sensed that she was answering his questions truthfully. Earlier that morning police officers who had been round to the other flats in the building where Semple lived, had been told by the tenants that the young woman on the second floor had frequently been heard arguing and shouting at the young man who sometimes spent the night there. It was the kind of information that neighbours volunteered only too readily in murder enquiries and by now, no doubt, they would have convinced themselves that Semple had killed the man in a jealous frenzy. Crawford was less easily convinced and after he had let Semple leave he went and reported to Forbes.

'You don't believe she killed him?' Forbes asked.

'No. Why should she?'

'Did she not say that she was expecting him for supper and he was nearly two hours late?'

'Oh, aye. She might have hit him when he got to the flat. She has a temper that one. But she'd wait to hear what excuse he had for his tardiness. She'd not have gone and attacked him on the stairs.'

'Did she know about his condition?'

'It seems so.'

'Then you could be right. Why should a spinster of her age knock off a potential husband?'

'That's true,' Crawford agreed but he did not appear wholly convinced with Forbes's line of reasoning and added, 'On the other hand it's a strange thing, but though the lassie was obviously fond of the man and is upset about his death without a doubt, I've the feeling she's not sorry to be rid of him.'

'In what way?'

'She had got herself locked in with the man, trapped in a relationship which was starting to get on her nerves, from which she wished to escape but which her pride demanded should end in marriage.'

'Too deep for me. Head-shrinker stuff,' Forbes said, but he had a respect for Crawford's judgement, especially in the matter of women. After all, the man had managed to divorce two wives and acquire a

113

third, all on a policeman's salary.

'I'm coming round to believing that whoever used that bottle on the dead man was only working out a grudge; wanted to spoil the pretty boy's looks.'

'Ah! He'd been sniffing around someone else's bit of skirt, had he?' That was an uncomplicated motive for violence which Forbes could understand.

'Someone else's? Everyone else's! The man was a pathological womanizer. From debs to detectives' daughters, he couldn't leave them alone. He seemed to have to prove his virility.'

'Could be he'd settled for a short life and wished to cram as many women as he could into it. You know, die on the job with a smile on his face.'

'Maybe. Whatever it was he was bound to find trouble. A few weeks ago he was being done over by a bunch of neds with brass knuckles outside some pub and was saved by one of our patrol cars.'

'So what do you want to do?'

'Find out where he was last evening before he went up to the Semple woman's place. I've sent some men out already to make enquiries. It shouldn't be too difficult. Then maybe we'll learn where he started the aggro and why.'

'Meantime you've let the woman go?'

'Aye. We know where we can find her. But the man Sanderson who's staying with her is still here.'

'What for?'

'I thought you'd maybe like a word with him. It was him who told them down at Stranraer that the body on the foreshore was MacNair's.'

'Was it indeed?'

'Yes and last evening he was having dinner with MacNair's daughter in Edinburgh. That's what he told me and he's not likely to have made it up, knowing we could easily check.'

'I find that very interesting.'

'He says that when MacNair disappeared the girl asked him to see if he could find out what had happened to him.'

Forbes turned the scrap of information over in his mind, suspiciously like a wino examining a half-full bottle of Scotch he had found

114

in a dustbin. 'They say MacNair was a wealthy man. The girl's an only child and this Sanderson is out of a job.'

'Are you thinking that the two of them might have murdered her father?'

'It's been known before. The girl wasn't very close to her father. She hadn't seen him for years.'

'Yes, but isn't Sanderson shacked up with this Semple woman?'

'Very likely, but that needn't make any difference. You know how young people behave today; changing partners, going to bed in threes, group sex, gang bangs!' Forbes shook his head. He was a son of the manse and had inherited some of his father's disapproval of moral laxity. 'It's like Scottish country dancing gone mad!'

By a coincidence Sanderson, while he was waiting in another room, was also thinking of sex. The memory of Maggie's nakedness still lingered, as pervasive and as disquieting as a late-night Tandoori meal. When he had awoken that morning she had no longer been lying next to him and he could hear her moving around noisily and, it seemed, cheerfully in the bathroom. His first reaction had been one of self-reproach for his lack of willpower. He had no wish to become emotionally involved with Maggie. It was far too late; far too much had happened since the first flush of adolescent passion. But he had given in to temptation and things would never be the same again. Maggie would make demands to which he could not respond and he would have to find somewhere else to live.

As he lay in bed he had realized without any pleasure that he would soon have to face her and wondered what she would do and say and how he should handle it. But when eventually they met over the breakfast table, Maggie had given no sign that she even remembered their love-making. She had talked without emotion of Simon's death, asking Sanderson whether she should telephone Simon's parents and if so, how she could find a number where she could reach them. They were holidaying in Greece apparently and had left Simon a copy of their itinerary. The two of them had breakfasted late and had not finished when they had a call from C.I.D. headquarters asking them if they would both be kind enough to go down there, as Inspector Crawford had further questions to ask them. On the way to Pitt Street

115

Maggie, nervous and ill-at-ease, had scarcely spoken at all and consequently neither of them had yet mentioned what had happened in bed the previous night.

Now, sitting waiting in police headquarters, Sanderson realized that they would not be able to go on indefinitely ignoring the incident. Maggie, in spite of her vocal support for the equality of the sexes, would expect him as a man to make the first mention of such an intimate matter and he had no idea of what she would wish him to say. He had reached no conclusion when a police constable arrived and led him to a room where Crawford was waiting with another officer who introduced himself as Chief Inspector Forbes.

'I'm sorry to have kept you waiting, sir,' Forbes said. 'Would you like a cup of tea?'

'No, thanks. I don't go much for tea,' Sanderson replied, wondering why the British had come to believe in the universal efficacy of tea for almost any purpose and dispensed it liberally in police stations, hospitals and other institutions where people might be suffering from anxiety, grief or fear.

'I understand you have not long moved to Glasgow from London.'

'Yes. I came back to Scotland when I lost my job down there.'

'What was your occupation in London, sir?'

'I worked for a firm of management consultants.'

'Is it true that last night you were in Edinburgh having dinner with the daughter of the late Mr Iain MacNair?' Forbes did not wait for Sanderson to reply, but asked, 'May I ask where you had dinner?'

'At a restaurant called Prestonfield House.'

'I see.' Sanderson seemed to sense in the remark the merest hint of surprise that an unemployed young man should take a girl to such an up-market restaurant. 'And after dinner you took her home no doubt?'

'I did and she invited me in for a cup of coffee.'

'How long would you have spent there?'

'Half an hour, maybe forty minutes.' Forbes's questions were beginning to irritate Sanderson and he wondered whether all innocent people who were questioned by the police felt the same.

'Another young woman lives with Miss MacNair, does she not?'

'Yes, she shares the flat with a friend.'

'Was this young woman there when you went in for coffee?'

'No, she was not.'

Forbes made no comment. That and the short silence which followed managed to convey his suspicion that Sanderson might be lying, that he and Katriona might have conspired to provide Sanderson with an alibi. Then he remarked, 'You have not known Miss MacNair for long.'

'No, for only a few days.'

'And how did you come to meet her?'

Once again Sanderson had to tell the story of how he had met MacNair while hill walking in Wester Ross and how after his return Katriona had telephoned to tell him of her father's disappearance. The story was beginning to seem both interminable and boring to him, but Forbes listened attentively, asking more questions. Deftly, one by one, he drew out scraps of information which Sanderson had not intended to give him, not through secrecy but because he could not see their relevance to the death of Simon; MacNair's claim that someone was trying to have him killed, the trip to Speyside from which he had apparently never returned home, Sanderson's suspicion that MacNair's filing cabinet of private papers had been forcibly broken open.

'You've not been idle, have you Mr Sanderson?' Forbes said when he had finished. 'That's a deal of information you've collected.'

'Too much, perhaps.'

'Why do you say that?'

'Is it not possible that last night my friend Simon was murdered by mistake?'

'By mistake, sir?'

'Yes, I believe that whoever attacked Simon thought he was me.'

Forbes showed no interest in the suggestion. All he said was, 'Your friend was not murdered.'

'Not murdered?'

'At the most it would only be a charge of manslaughter. That blow on the head would not have killed anyone, but your friend had a heart complaint. Aortic Stenosis is the medical name for it but you and I would probably know it as a heart murmur. His doctor says he had rheumatic fever as a lad and one often follows the other.'

117

Hearing that Simon had not been murdered filled Sanderson with a feeling which now he recognized as relief because Maggie would not be charged with murder. The knowledge that in spite of what he had told her the previous night, in spite of what he had told himself at frequent intervals since, in spite of logic and common sense, part of him could still believe that she might have killed Simon annoyed Sanderson. He said to Forbes sharply, 'In that case I can't see the relevance of all the questions you have been asking me.'

'Sir?'

'You made it appear as though you suspected me of murdering Simon.'

Forbes put on a show of seeming puzzled. 'You must be mistaken, sir. I'm not concerned with the death of your friend.'

'You're not?'

'No. I'm investigating the murder of Mr Iain MacNair.'

## 14

THAT EVENING SANDERSON walked into the centre of Glasgow. He walked at a leisurely pace, turning off Great Western Road soon after he had left the flat and then taking any turning that appealed to him, exploring parts of the city which he did not know at all, passing through streets of dilapidated houses and struggling shops whose makeshift signboards showed how often they had changed hands.

The traffic was light even as he approached the centre and there were few people to be seen. Sanderson was not surprised for he had noticed the change in Glasgow as soon as he arrived back from London. It saddened him for he felt he was watching the slow death of a great city. The slums of the Gorbals had been demolished, Victorian buildings had been replaced with new offices and hotels which, from a distance, looked as though they had been constructed out of a child's building blocks, the rooftops had been festooned with a long macadam ribbon of motorway. The gangs which controlled the underworld had been destroyed, the worst of the vice eradicated, Glasgow had been cleaned up morally as well as architecturally but the people had left. Each year the population diminished perceptibly. Now Sauchiehall Street on Saturday night was lifeless and cheerless, a ghost of the legend it had been.

And why should the people stay? The shipyards were silent, the docks almost empty, the engineering shops and the steel mills dismantled. To watch the decline of a once proud and important city was sad but what saddened Sanderson more was that no one appeared to care.

He had spent that afternoon alone in the flat, for Maggie had gone straight from police headquarters to the offices of the *Chronicle*. A letter had arrived that morning from a management selection firm telling him of one of their client companies which was looking for a

119

production director and asking him if he would like to be considered for the job. The company manufactured highly specialized paints and protective coatings in the Midlands of England and it was a job for which Sanderson was well qualified. He would have preferred to work in Scotland but, conscious of how long he had now been without work, he had replied that afternoon telling them that he was interested.

Later Maggie had telephoned to say she would be dining out that evening. He had been secretly relieved for he still had no means of knowing how their intimacy of the previous night had affected her feelings for him. Would she expect that from now on she could come to his bed whenever she chose and if she did come how was he to refuse her? Without disapproving of casual sex, he had never cared much for it and he certainly had no wish for any form of permanent relationship with Maggie. The only thought which gave him any comfort was that perhaps she might well feel the same and that was why she was staying out, to avoid having to dine alone with him.

After crossing the underpass through which the motorway passed at Charing Cross, he made his way towards the Clyde, for he intended to have his supper in a Chinese restaurant which he knew in Argyle Street. Near the bus station at Anderston Cross he looked back as he was crossing the street and noticed a man in a green tweed suit some distance away but walking in the same direction as he was. When he looked round the man seemed to check his stride, hesitating as though he had remembered something he should be doing and was thinking of turning back. Instantly Sanderson was alert. Earlier when he had looked out of the window of the flat to see whether the weather was still fine, he had seen a man in a green suit walking slowly along the opposite side of the street, and, it seemed, glancing up towards Maggie's window from time to time. He remembered the attack on Simon the previous evening, but did not look back again. From what he had seen in one quick glance the man in green did not look built for violence, thin and far from robust and well dressed in an unostentatious way, but Sanderson wanted to make sure.

Passing by the bus station, he turned into Argyle Street and walked eastwards, through the tunnel under the Central Station and turning left soon afterwards towards Buchanan Street. He did not look back

120

again but once, glancing in a shop window that faced him, he saw a reflection of the street behind him and was almost certain that among the people on the busy pavement was the figure of a man in green.

Not far from St Enoch Square he came up to the entrance of a pub and on a sudden impulse went inside. If when he came out again the man in green was still anywhere to be seen, then he would know without any doubt that he was being followed.

Inside he found an old traditional Glasgow pub in which 50 years previously a woman would never have been seen, but which had made an effort to adapt itself to the more discerning tastes of the contemporary drinking public with shaded lights, plastic-topped bar stools, plastic-topped tables, bar snacks which might easily have been mistaken for plastic, video games and canned music. The smell of the disinfectant with which the floor had been scrubbed that morning still lingered.

He bought himself a whisky at the bar and took it to an empty table in the far corner of the room. Ten or fifteen minutes, he decided, would be enough to make the man in green show his hand. He was in no hurry. The alarm which he had felt when he saw the man in the street behind him had subsided, leaving only a strange, subdued excitement.

He had taken only two sips from his whisky when to his surprise the man in green came into the room, walked straight to the bar and ordered a drink. Sanderson watched him. He stood by the bar, looking straight ahead of him and not turning or moving his head, like a bad actor following stage instructions which stipulated that he should enter a room casually, without noticing another character in the scene.

As a performance it was so stilted that Sanderson wanted to laugh. Then he had a better idea. Taking his whisky with him, he went up to the bar and tapped the man on the shoulder. The man looked around, so startled that he spilt some of his drink on to the bar counter.

'Why are you following me?' The question was direct and demanding but he made it with a friendly smile.

'I don't know what you mean! I'm not following anyone. I've never seen you before.' The words rolled out, propelled by panic.

There was no way, Sanderson decided, that the man could be a professional thug. Although he could not have been much past fifty, he had the dry, brittle look of impending age, fluttering hands and thick spectacles.

'Are you a private detective?'

'Certainly not! I'm a lawyer.'

It was then that Sanderson remembered where he had seen the man before. 'You were in C.I.D. headquarters this morning,' he said accusingly. 'I saw you coming out.'

'All right. What if I was?' the man replied, looking round nervously as though afraid that other people might have heard his admission.

'Look, let's sit down and talk,' Sanderson said persuasively. 'Bring your drink with you. No, better still, I'll buy you another. Whisky isn't it?' He turned to the barman. 'Two MacNair's Gold Label, please.'

'Not MacNair's. Any other brand but that!'

The barman poured two measures from another of the Scotches which he had up on optics and Sanderson led the man in green back to the table where he had been sitting before. If the man had not changed his clothes since that morning he might have recognized him sooner. Then he had been wearing a black jacket, striped trousers and a bowler hat.

'What's this all about?'

'My name's Gough,' the man replied, as though that were a sufficient explanation.

'Oh, yes?'

'The police think I murdered Iain MacNair.'

'And did you?'

'Of course not! Why should I wish to kill him?'

Sanderson looked at Gough. So the man was a lawyer and would not drink MacNair's whisky. He remembered a remark which Peter Wandercliff had made the first time he had met him. A lawyer working for the North British Brewery had been dismissed for negligence in drawing up an agreement when MacNair had left the company.

'Did you lose your job over MacNair?' he asked.

'Oh my God! Does everyone know?' Gough's whole face seemed to sag with despair. 'And now you believe I killed him as well!'

122

'No I don't. Not for a moment.' Sanderson meant what he said. The idea that Gough might be a ruthless and clever murderer was absurd.

'MacNair was very good to me.'

'In that way?'

'As the police probably told you, I was distraught when the brewery fired me. I blamed MacNair and wrote him abusive letters, but he refused to prosecute when the police found out I was responsible. And he helped me in other ways.'

Gough explained that MacNair had tried unsuccessfully to persuade the North British Brewery to reinstate him. Then he learnt that part of the reason for Gough's despair was that the lawyer was in acute financial difficulties, owing a large sum of money to a bookmaker but having no income and no savings. MacNair had helped him, paid off his debts and made him a loan to cover his expenses until he found another job.

'Why should I kill him?' Gough repeated. 'The man saved my marriage, my home, my life.' Sanderson must have shown by his expression that he felt that this was an exaggeration, for Gough went on, 'It's true! The bookmaker had already sent a man round to threaten me. A thug named Bryce. There was no doubt that he meant business. It was like the old days of the razor gangs in Glasgow.'

'Who was the bookie?' Sanderson was suddenly curious.

'One of the big Glasgow bookmakers. Jock Ferguson.'

Gough was past restraint, carried away by his need to talk. Words, confidences, grievances, indignation flowed out, affording him all the relief of a strong and badly needed purgative. He told Sanderson about his work at the brewery, how his opinions had been ignored, his advice treated with contempt, the anger of his superiors when they saw how MacNair had outwitted them. Sanderson listened, not because he was interested, but because it seemed a charitable thing to do. He also bought Gough another whisky, justifying it with the thought that perhaps it was bread upon the waters and he might still learn something of value. The reward came sooner than he expected.

'Why were you following me?' he asked Gough.

'I wanted to speak to you; to find out how much you knew about MacNair's death.'

'Very little really.'

123

'Do you know that his wife divorced him and that he hadn't seen his daughter for years?' Gough hopped from one question to another at random. For a lawyer his thought processes were strangely unpredictable. When Sanderson nodded he continued, 'MacNair and I became quite friendly. He took me out to lunch once. That was when he told me about young Robertson.'

'Who's Robertson?'

'Katriona's young man. One day he went to MacNair and asked him for fifty thousand. Said he wished to start his own business.'

'Did MacNair let him have the money?'

'He told me that he very nearly did. He doted on his daughter, you see, even though she ignored him. Then he decided to make a few discreet enquiries and found out Robertson was a cheat and a liar, that he'd borrowed money before and was heavily in debt. So he refused.'

'What happened?'

'Robertson turned very unpleasant. Threatened he'd walk out on Katriona. They had been living together, you understand. He told MacNair the girl couldn't live without him. But MacNair still refused.'

'Why are you telling me all this?' Sanderson asked.

'Can't you see? Now Katriona will inherit all MacNair's money and give Robertson whatever he wants.'

After eating his Chinese meal, Sanderson dropped into another pub on his way back to the flat. In the restaurant he had thought a good deal about what Gough had told him. That Katriona should have shacked up with a man did not surprise him for she was an attractive girl, financially independent and independent in her views as well, but one would suppose that living with a fellow whom presumably she loved would have made her less defensive and suspicious, more relaxed and more fulfilled. It might be that the relationship she was sharing was not a very happy one. He wondered whether her motive in inviting her father to dinner had been to persuade him to give Robertson the money he wanted and even whether she had ever invited him. The story could have been just an invention.

Wanting more time to think he went into the pub and ordered a

124

malt whisky. There was a large colour television set in the bar and he saw that the news had just started. In the assured, well modulated tones of one who was impervious to disasters, the newscaster was dispensing the day's ration of gloomy stories from the Middle East, South America and the Caribbean and repeating extracts of hysterical abuse by trade union leaders against the Government at home. While Sanderson listened he made a more local announcement.

'A report has just been received that a major fire has broken out in the premises of a whisky company in Cumbernauld. The extent of the fire is not yet known but it is understood that several fire engines are on the scene and are attempting to get the blaze under control.'

Hurrying from the pub, he found a taxi at the Central Station which took him to where his car was parked outside Maggie's place and then drove to Cumbernauld. As he had anticipated the fire was at the Loch Rannoch Whisky Company, but it was by no means as sensational as the television reports had suggested. It had been confined to the office building and by the time Sanderson arrived the flames had been extinguished and the firemen were doing no more than directing their hoses from time to time on smouldering debris which threatened to erupt into a blaze again. Even so, half a dozen newspaper reporters and two television crews were still there, reluctant to accept that this was not the devastating whisky fire which everyone in Strathclyde had been expecting for years.

The lingering fear that any day Glasgow would be destroyed when hundreds of thousands of gallons of whisky lying in the city's warehouses accidently caught fire dated back to March 1960 and the infamous Cheapside fire. Nineteen firemen had been killed fighting the fire at a whisky warehouse and ever since that time every fire, however small, which broke out anywhere in the vicinity of a whisky bond provoked panic in the media and immediate reports of disaster. Now, although almost all the major whisky companies had built themselves blending and bottling halls and warehouses outside of Glasgow and there were few bonds holding any significant amounts of whisky left inside the city boundaries, the fear persisted in much the same way as San Francisco still waits in trepidation for its next earthquake.

Among the newspaper men there Sanderson recognized a reporter from the *Glasgow Chronicle* whom he had once met when he and Maggie were out with Simon. He went over to the man and asked him whether the cause of the fire was known.

'They'll not know definitely until the experts have examined the place, but a fireman friend of mine who was one of the first out here is certain it was no accident.'

'Then it was arson?'

'Aye. The fire seems to have started with an explosion in a room where all the firm's records were kept.'

'A bomb?'

'Likely a home-made fire bomb set off by a timing device. It could have been planted hours before.'

Leaving the reporter, Sanderson went to search for Peter Wandercliff and found him talking to a senior officer in the fire brigade and an inspector from the local constabulary. He waited until the three men had finished their conversation and then intercepted Wandercliff as he moved away.

'Bruce!' Wandercliff exclaimed. 'So you got my message?'

'What message?'

'I asked my secretary to let you know as soon as I was told about the fire.'

'When did it start?'

'Two or three hours ago, I should think. Fortunately the security people who look after the place came by on a routine patrol and spotted the flames in the office.'

'So not much damage was done?'

Wandercliff appeared offended by Sanderson's indifference. 'All our files and office records have been destroyed. That may not seem very important but do you realize what might easily have happened? The whole place could have gone up! There are several thousands of gallons of whisky in the blending vats and hundreds of cases already bottled and packed awaiting shipment.'

'Everything's insured of course?'

'Of course, but that's not the point. That whisky could not be replaced overnight. The different malts and grains which we use in our blends are simply not available in the quantities which we would require. So we would not be able to meet the orders we have and our customers would go elsewhere. We might well lose the business for ever. Don't you understand? First Iain is murdered, then they try to burn down our bond. Someone is determined to destroy our business.'

'Why should anyone wish to do that?'

'Iain seems to have made any number of enemies in the whisky trade. I'm finding that out now. While I was away on honeymoon he managed to upset many of his old friends.'

'How did you find out?'

'Douglass Tweedie called me at home last evening.'

Sir Douglass, according to Wandercliff, had described how Iain MacNair's attempts to have the legal definition of whisky changed had annoyed and alarmed folk in the trade. They thought that what he intended was to flood the market with immature spirit 'tarted up', as Tweedie put it, to look like genuine whisky. Even though nobody really believed that the Government would agree to the definition being changed, they were afraid that MacNair had other schemes in mind which would debase the quality and the image of Scotch, that were so important to its worldwide success.

'And Douglass is right,' Wandercliff said. 'We whisky men are not mere producers of booze, mere producers of drinks like gin and vodka which can be distilled today and sold tomorrow. We are the custodians of a great heritage, of an art which has been passed down from one generation to the next for centuries, of a drink which demands time, patience and great skill in its making and which, for that reason, is the finest spirit drink in the world.'

The words, Sanderson realized, might be coming from Wandercliff, but they had been put into his mouth by Sir Douglass with a persuasiveness and suggestion as skilful as any ventriloquist's art. One could see why Wandercliff would be so susceptible to such manipulation. A man who had copied his adopted country's manners, dress and speech so faithfully must be in love with it. Wandercliff would never have been able to resist an appeal to what he would see as a typically British sense of responsibility.

'Did Sir Douglass ask you to abandon Iain MacNair's plans?' he asked.

'He suggested as much and I believe he is right. In any case I can't develop Iain's process because I have no idea what it was and he appears to have left no notes or instructions.'

Shortly afterwards Sanderson left Cumbernauld. There seemed to be nothing useful to be learned at the scene of the fire and he was only curious to know why Wandercliff had apparently wanted him to go out there. One day he might ask him.

As he drove back to Glasgow, he thought too about Wandercliff's remark that MacNair had left no notes or other details of his process of accelerated maturation. A man as suspicious and paranoid as MacNair might well be afraid of putting anything down in writing in case it might be stolen, but on the other hand the files which MacNair had left showed that he was methodical in his work and left nothing to chance. He would surely have made notes on the experiments he had tried if only for his own guidance. Perhaps there had been notes and perhaps they had been stolen from his files or wherever else he had concealed them.

Remembering the evening they had spent together in the mountain bothy, he recalled MacNair's suspicion and hostility when he had found Sanderson already in the place, the questions he had asked, what he had said about the process which was going to transform the whisky business and about the attempts on his life. He could not help thinking that somewhere in what the man had said or hinted there should be a clue to the real reason why he had been murdered. It was familiar ground, for he had often thought about that night before, but once again nothing startling emerged.

While parking his car outside Maggie's apartment he was reassured to notice a uniformed policeman not more than 50 yards away along the street. When the man reached the corner of the street he turned and began to walk back, like a sentry on duty. It was the sound of his boots scraping on the pavement that triggered off Sanderson's memory. He remembered a similar sound, only louder and more prolonged, which he had heard when he awoke that night in the bothy; the sound of scratching or digging on hard, compacted soil.

Upstairs in the apartment, although it was past midnight, he went to the telephone and dialled Katriona's number. It rang for a long time unanswered but finally he heard her sleepy voice.

'Tomorrow morning I'm driving up to the bothy where I met your father,' he told her. 'Will you come with me?'

The lights were on in the living-room and stale cigar smoke hung and drifted in the air. A half-empty bottle of whisky and two glasses stood on a coffee table by the sofa. When he was passing Maggie's bedroom he noticed that a piece of paper had been pinned on the door with a flippant message written in what looked like a tipsy scrawl.

DO NOT DISTURB
Very private meeting in progress!

Like anyone else would have done, he paused outside the door to listen. He heard a man's voice, followed by Maggie's gasps and cries of pleasure.

## 15

'I WISH I had seen my father again before he died,' Katriona said suddenly.

'Are you saying that you wish you had gone to your mother's dinner party?'

'Not at all. But I had the opportunity of getting in touch with him some months ago. I was too stubborn or too proud or perhaps just too stupid to take it.'

'When was that?'

'My firm wanted information about whisky for an American client and Peter Strachan, one of my colleagues, knowing who my father was, suggested I should ask him for it.'

She told Sanderson how an American businessman named Marshall Friend had come to seek her firm's advice on whisky which his father had bought some years previously. 'He was sure it was a swindle, that there was no whisky and that his father had been sold a worthless scrap of paper,' she added.

'But he was wrong?'

'Yes. In the end he was very pleased with the outcome.'

'What happened?'

'We arranged for the whisky to be bottled for him under a personal label and had it shipped back to the States for his private use. I would think he has enough to last him and his friends for five years at least.'

Katriona had met Sanderson by arrangement that morning outside Stirling and, leaving her car in a public car park, they had set out in his for Wester Ross through Crianlarich, Glencoe and Fort William. Sanderson knew from what she had told him when they dined together in Edinburgh that Katriona had only once been north of Pitlochry, and he realized that she knew nothing of the Highlands and their history except what every Scottish child is taught at school.

So he began pointing out landmarks to her, diffidently at first, not wishing to sound patronizing or to parade his knowledge. Gradually, though, the interest which she showed and the questions she asked broke down his reticence. This was the country which had been his home and soon, carried away with pride and affection, he was drawing Katriona's attention to the unspoilt beauty of the landscape, the silent lochs lying beneath protective hills, burns which tumbled down heather-covered slopes or cascaded over rock faces, silent peaks, austere and majestic, the spectacular views which followed each other around almost every bend in the road.

He told her too of the history in which that whole part of Scotland was steeped. Just north of Fort William they passed the battlefield of Inverlochy where the Marquis of Montrose with a small royalist force drawn from the Donald, Cameron and Stewart clans had routed a covenanting army of 5,000 Campbells in 1645 after a forced march in winter which was one of the great feats of military history, a march and a victory only made possible by the clansmen's hatred of the Campbells.

'Were the Campbells really detested?' Katriona asked.

'The hatred still lingers. If I meet a man of that name today I find myself, well, not actually recoiling but holding back, wary and suspicious.'

'One would not expect to find that kind of unscientific prejudice in a management consultant,' Katriona said, and laughed.

'I know, but I can't help it. It's in the blood.'

After crossing the Caledonian Canal to the west side of Loch Oich, Sanderson pointed out the Tobar nan Ceann, or Well of the Heads, a pyramid on a square column which carried a cluster of men's heads at its summit. It was a monument, he told her, commemorating the terrible vengeance taken for the treacherous murder of the young clan chief MacDonald of Keppoch and his brother by seven men of a rival clan while they were guests at his home. The heads of the murderers were laid at the feet of the high chief of the clan at Glengarry Castle, after first being washed at the well where the monument was later erected. A short distance further along the road they passed the ruins of Glengarry Castle itself, which had been burned down by the Duke of Cumberland because it had given shelter to Prince Charles after the battle of Culloden.

'Why is it, I wonder,' Katriona remarked thoughtfully, 'that violence dominates the history of our country?'

Sanderson made no reply to what he supposed was a rhetorical question and presently they turned off the Inverness road at Invergarry and drove along Loch Cluanie, before stopping for a bar lunch at the Cluanie Inn. It was early for lunch and the car park of the inn was empty except for a dirty brown Porsche, a plumber's van and an ancient Mini. The main bar in which they had their lunch was also deserted except for the young barman and their food was served in a few minutes.

While they were eating Katriona returned to the subject of Scottish history. 'Scotland has given so much to science and industry and art,' she said. 'Think of Watt and Stevenson and Adam and Fleming and Baird. Has any other nation so small made a greater contribution to civilization? But our heroes are William Wallace and Robert the Bruce and Montrose and a score of others who fought to preserve our independence and usually fought in vain.'

'Most people don't think of either science or art as particularly heroic.'

She appeared not to have heard his reply but continued, 'And most of the violence in our history has been inspired by a passion for revenge. Think of all the folk, many of them humble and quite harmless, who were hunted down and butchered just because they had given shelter or aid to Prince Charles Edward.'

'That was the Duke of Cumberland's doing.'

'You know as well as I do that a large number of his men were Scots. At Culloden it was Scot against Scot. The old clan hatreds were stronger than hatred of the common enemy, the English. Old grievances must be avenged, old scores settled, old wrongs righted and always with the sword. That has been the tragedy of Scotland.'

Sanderson was not disposed to argue, but much of what she had said was true. Legends of violent and heroic deeds, of savage bravery and treachery and revenge overshadowed the history of Scotland like the clouds which so often hung oppressively over the glens in the Highlands through which they were passing. He found himself wondering, though, what had provoked Katriona's mood. She had given him the impression of being a girl who was totally sure of the values she had placed on life, but now her observations seemed not so much a commentary on the Scottish character as an essay in self-analysis.

As though to confirm his line of speculation she remarked, 'It makes me wonder about my own motives.'

'What motives?'

'My motives for wanting to know who killed my father. Is it just a wish that whoever did kill him should be punished, a thirst for revenge? Look at it dispassionately. I wasn't close to my father. I never saw him for years and that didn't bother me overmuch. It was only when I learnt how my mother had treated him that I took any interest in him.'

'And then you wanted to make amends for the unhappiness you felt you had caused him? That doesn't sound unreasonable.'

'Perfectly reasonable, if that was all I wanted.'

'What else did you want?'

Katriona did not reply at once and Sanderson sensed that she had a confession to make but could not summon up the courage to step into the confessional. Eventually she said, 'Perhaps I'm hoping that I can expiate my feeling of guilt with revenge.'

'Revenge on whom?'

'My mother.'

'Does that mean you believe it was she who had your father murdered?' he asked bluntly.

She shook her head unhappily. 'I can't decide whether I really believe she and Jock were responsible or whether I just hope they were.'

When they left the inn and were following the road which plunged down into Glen Shiel in broad, sweeping curves, the sky which had been bright and clear all the way from Stirling began to darken as clouds appeared, sombre and grey, to shroud the mountain peaks. To the north the undulating ridge of the Five Sisters of Kintail was soon enveloped. To the south they were permitted a final glimpse of the majestic Saddle, brooding like a Highland Matterhorn above the sharp-fanged spine of the Forcan ridge. Sanderson wondered whether time was playing tricks and if, as they climbed the hills, they would have an exact repetition of the sudden rainstorm which had driven first him and then Iain MacNair into the mountain bothy. This time, though, the wind was not from the west but from the north-east, and soon he was sure it would sweep the clouds away.

They drove through the glen, past Shiel Bridge, parked the Mercedes off the road not far from Morvich and set off inland on foot, following the river Croe. When Katriona had agreed to drive up to Wester Ross with him the previous night, he had advised her to come dressed for walking and she was wearing tweed slacks and a wind-proof anorak. He was also glad to see that she had chosen a pair of sturdy walking shoes, for they would have at least three miles to cover through rough and boggy country to reach the bothy and maybe a mile more if he decided to avoid the steepest route.

After a time they turned away from the river, followed a burn which came tumbling down the hillside in a series of small waterfalls, turned again to climb a wooded slope and cross a ridge and then began a long, gradual descent towards the copse of trees by which the bothy stood. The clouds had lifted and patches of blue sky began to appear above them.

Sanderson was drawn to the silence and solitude even more than the wild splendour of what they saw, reminding him as they did of his childhood and pushing back more recent memories of violence and anger and frustration and of the banal pleasures of the life he had been leading, until they receded and became meaningless. He was curious to know how the experience was affecting Katriona. With her city upbringing she would not feel the nostalgia that was tugging at his emotions, but even so he could not believe that she would be completely unmoved. He would have asked her but was afraid that she might spoil his own pleasure with a trite or commonplace reply.

As it was a Sunday, he had expected that there might be others walking the hills or fishing, but they saw no one. The bothy when they reached it looked a good deal less attractive than it had in a rainstorm, with the pale afternoon sunlight exposing its dilapidation as cruelly as arc lights show off the flaws in a woman's skin, however carefully she may camouflage them. Sanderson was glad to find no one inside to watch inquisitively as he began digging up the hard earth floor.

They had brought a garden trowel with them, the only suitable implement he had been able to find at Maggie's home. Sanderson knew of no place in Glasgow where he could have bought or borrowed a spade early on a Sunday morning. After showing Katriona the layout of the bothy, he pointed out the bunk on which he had been lying when he woke and heard what he had since decided was the noise made by her father digging in the floor. The noise had come from the other room and they decided that if they had something which they wished to hide, they would choose one of the corners of the room, partly because any traces of digging would be less likely to be noticed there and partly because the soil would be less compacted in the corners of the rooms.

'Your father would probably have selected one of the corners on the far side of the room, surely,' Sanderson said, 'so that the noise he made would be less likely to waken me.'

'Unless he wanted to wake you; for you to hear the noise and be curious.'

'Good thinking!'

He began digging in the corner of the room which was nearest to where he had been sleeping. Although it was well trodden down, the ground was not as hard as he had expected. He worked evenly over an area of about eighteen inches by eighteen, gradually making a shallow pit, uncertain what size of object he might expect to find.

'Now I understand something my father said in that letter he wrote me,' Katriona remarked when Sanderson paused for a rest.

'What was that?'

'There was a lot in the letter about you; what a fine young man you were and how my father hoped he might be able to persuade Peter Wandercliff to take you into their business. Then right at the end he said something which I decided was a piece of flippant nonsense. "Tell young Sanderson," he wrote, "that sometimes the hills can be made to give up their secrets." That was all.'

'A pity you didn't tell me that before. It might have saved us time and spared us some aggro.'

'It seemed unimportant so I just put it out of my mind.'

Sanderson resumed his digging. When the pit was about six inches deep, the trowel struck a hard object. After they had cleared away a little more soil with their hands, they saw that it was a tin which had once held stewing steak. His first reaction was one of disappointment. Perhaps as he had thought when he had heard MacNair digging that night, the man had only been burying the rubbish from their meal. Then he saw that the tin had been carefully wrapped in the remains of a cellophane packet and he recognized it as one he had bought from a village shop during his hill walk.

'Buried treasure,' he exclaimed. 'Your father opened this can when he was preparing our supper that evening.'

The lid of the can had been cut right off and when he took it out of its protective wrapper, he could see that it must also have been washed out and dried before being used as an improvised strongbox. Three sheets of paper had been folded lengthwise and rolled into a cylinder before being inserted in the can. He extracted them carefully and when he unrolled them, saw that they were covered in a small, neat handwriting.

'That's my father's writing,' Katriona said at once. 'I recognize it.'

'Now maybe we'll find out what this is all about.'

'Is there anything else in the tin? I thought I heard a knocking noise as you pulled the papers out.'

When Sanderson turned the can upside down a tiny cassette of recording tape, complete in its plastic container, fell into his hand. He recognized it as a tape for use in a micro-recorder similar to the one he had seen on the desk in MacNair's study, with a playing time of thirty minutes. Nothing was written on the plastic box or on the tape itself, so he slipped it into his trouser pocket.

'We'll leave that till later,' he told Katriona. 'First let's see what your father wrote.'

It was too gloomy inside the bothy to read MacNair's tiny writing with any degree of comfort, so they went outside, sat down on the grass in the sunshine and began to read the top sheet of the three.

THE SPIRIT OF SCOTLAND

*Production Plan and Marketing Strategy*

### The Product
The Spirit of Scotland will be the registered brand name for a high quality blend of whiskies, all of which will be treated by the MacNair

136

process of accelerated maturation. Since the whiskies will not conform to the legal definition of whisky presently laid down in the Finance Act, they will not be entitled to the description of whisky, so the label on the bottles will define them as 'A Blend of the finest Malt and Grain spirit, distilled, blended and bottled in Scotland.'

*The Blend*

Until further tests have been carried out it is not known how different single whiskies respond to the MacNair process of accelerated maturation. Some may be affected more favourably than others and some may prove to have a better character and flavour after treatment than they would have had after normal maturation. At this stage, therefore, it is not possible to decide on the selection and patterns of treatment of different single whiskies for the blend. At present it is envisaged that 22 Malts and three Grain whiskies will be used and provisional lists have been drawn up and locked away in a secure place.

*Marketing and Promotion*

Since the company's money will not be tied up for several years maturing the whiskies used in S.O.S., it will be able to market the brand at a price significantly below those of standard brands of Scotch whisky in both the home and export markets. Even though the brand will not be labelled as Scotch, *consumers will immediately identify it as tasting exactly like Scotch whisky.* Moreover, because only higher quality Malts will be used and because there will be a higher proportion of Malt whisky than in many standard brands, the consumer will soon become aware that S.O.S. has as fine a flavour and character as many of the well-known brands.

The flavour of S.O.S. will therefore be one of its major selling points; another will be its Scottish origins. The word 'spirit' in the name will also have an appeal because of its two meanings, conveying as it does the unquenchable spirit, courage and independence of the Scot. This will be fully exploited in the advertising and promotion of the product as is explained in the detailed plans for its launching and marketing which follow.

Sanderson had finished reading the first of the three sheets, but he could see by following the movement of Katriona's eyes as she looked over his shoulder, that she had still a few lines left to read. As he waited for her to finish, he looked up and his eye was caught by a glint of light from the hillside opposite them. The light seemed to flash for an instant, disappear and then flashed again. He realized instantly what it was for he had seen the same effect many times before; sunlight reflected from a polished surface that was moving intermittently. The hill was not wooded but dotted with rocks and a few scattered clumps of broom. Sanderson looked away at once, but casually and without haste.

'Don't look now,' he said to Katriona quietly as he took the top sheet of the three they were reading and placed it behind the other two, 'but we are being watched.'

'Watched? By whom?'

'I've no idea. Somebody hidden on the hill facing us. I saw the sun glint on his binoculars.'

'Are you sure?'

'Absolutely.'

Katriona stared at the sheet of paper he was holding in front of them but she was not reading. Presently she said, 'What should we do?'

'Get back to the car.' He did not wish to frighten her but he was almost certain that he had spotted another glint of light, this time from a shiny object other than the binoculars, an object lying in the grass. 'But we mustn't let on that we know we are being watched. First I'll go back into the bothy again as though I were going to fetch something. Wait for a couple of minutes after I've gone and then get up casually and walk round to the back of the bothy. They'll think you're going for a pee. Once you're out of sight on the other side, make for the trees by the burn and wait for me there.'

'All right.' She did not question his instructions and he wondered if she thought he was making a drama out of nothing.

Once inside the bothy, Sanderson stood well back against the far wall where he would not be seen by anyone on the hill even through binoculars, but from where he could see through the open doorway. The binoculars were still pointed in their direction, but held steadily now, the glint of light unwavering. Presently he saw Katriona get to her feet and set out round the side of the bothy towards the back.

After giving her enough time to reach the safety of the trees, he started to follow her. He had reached the doorway when he noticed the trowel which they had brought with them lying on the ground and without thinking stooped to pick it up. It was an automatic, almost a reflex action but it must have warned the watcher on the hill of what he planned to do. As he walked along the front wall of the bothy towards the corner, he heard the unmistakable rushing noise of the bullet as it passed, missing his head by no more than a few inches. It struck a projection in the stonework of the wall and ricocheted away with a frightening high-pitched whine. Only as he flung himself around the corner of the bothy did he hear the report of the rifle.

## 16

KATRIONA WAS WAITING for him among the trees and it struck Sanderson that she looked a good deal more composed than he felt. 'Was that a shot I heard?' she asked him.

'Yes. Whoever was watching us had brought his rifle along with him as well as his glasses.'

'But who could it be? And why did he fire at you?'

'We can talk about that later. For the time being let's concentrate on getting the hell out of here.'

Sanderson looked around them. The trees among which they were sheltering were small and sparse, a narrow belt which followed the course of the burn through the glen. One way of escape from the trap in which they had suddenly found themselves would have been down the glen towards the west, but the cover which the trees might afford would be too thin and too patchy. A marksman of even moderate ability would have been able to pick them off without difficulty. On the other side of the burn were the lower slopes of a mountain which he remembered crossing during his hill walk, but the name of which he could not recall. Most of the mountains in that region were gaunt and bare, grass-covered slopes rising to sharp peaks and broken only by patches of treacherous scree and rock faces too steep to be climbed except by experienced rock climbers.

On the lower slopes of the mountain which faced them, however, was a man-made forest; a plantation of conifers created some years previously by the Forestry Commission as part of its reafforestation of the Highlands. The trees were mature now and thick enough to provide excellent cover if Katriona and he could reach them. The edge of the plantation was perhaps 80 paces away, separated from them by a stretch of uneven ground dotted with clumps of broom and small boulders. If Katriona and he were to make a dash for the plantation, they might surprise the man with the rifle on the hill behind them. Even so, assuming he was still in the same spot, he would have time for at least one shot before they reached cover.

'We'll make a run for those trees,' he told her, pointing in the direction of the plantation. 'But we'll go separately, some distance apart. You make for a point straight in line with the peak of the mountain. I'll go further to the right. Let me start first, count to five and then run as fast as you can.'

He was wearing light-brown denim trousers and a brown sweater over a gaudy red and yellow checked shirt. Before he started running he took off the sweater and tied it by the sleeves around his waist. Then he left the trees by the burn on the run. The ground was not as rough as he had expected but even so he did not run flat out for the first 40 yards or so. Then when he judged that the sniper on the opposite hill would have spotted him, he quickened his pace to a sprint, changing direction and swerving from one side to another every few paces.

He was not more than a few yards from the first line of trees when the bullet passed him and thudded into the bark of a spruce. But his judgement of time and speed had not been at fault and before the marksman could fire again he reached safety. As he crashed into the plantation he looked over his shoulder and saw that Katriona, taking a shorter route and running straight, had reached cover at almost the same moment. He paused to regain his breath and then picked his way between the closely planted trees towards her.

'You took your sweater off so that you would be seen,' she said accusingly when he reached her. 'So that you would be fired at and not me!'

'That's only partly true. I took it off because I wanted to make sure that the comedian with the rifle would see us and know where we were heading.'

'But why?'

'We must make him follow us. Otherwise he can go down the glen, find a convenient hiding place and pick us off when we get near the car.'

'Then what is your plan?'

Sanderson wanted to know her answer to a question of his own before he replied to Katriona's. 'How is your head for heights?'

'All right. I'm the one who has to go up ladders back in our flat. Why?'

'There is another way back to the car. Over that ridge.' He pointed towards a ridge on one side and below the summit of the mountain on whose slopes they were sheltering. 'But we must get our friend with the rifle to follow us to the crest. Then we'll drop down the other side, run to the car and be away before he reaches the bottom. Are you willing to give it a go?'

Katriona looked at him defiantly, as though his question implied that a woman might flinch from such a challenging and dangerous venture. 'Of course!'

Although the young forest was not much more than 300 yards wide, it was dense, and there were deep furrows between the rows of trees. They both stumbled frequently as they fought their way, pushing the branches aside. It was part of Sanderson's plan that the man with the rifle would guess where they were heading and would be watching for them to break cover on the other side of the plantation.

When they arrived at the far edge of the plantation, he pointed out to Katriona the ridge which he planned that they should cross. The slope up to it was much steeper than the land they had been crossing and grew progressively steeper nearer the crest of the ridge.

'We'll never be able to run up that,' she remarked.

'No. We'll just have to scramble up as fast as we can.'

'Won't we be very exposed?'

'Yes, but by this time we're beyond the range of that rifle.'

He decided that once again they would cross the open ground separately, some distance apart and he picked out a shorter path for Katriona, pointing out the spot at which she should aim to cross the ridge. He would go for a point further up towards the summit of the mountain and they would meet on the other side of the ridge to plan their descent.

They set out, running for as long as possible and then, when the ground grew too steep and too rocky, clambering over it as best they could. Sanderson was aware that what he had said about their being out of the marksman's range was only true if he had remained on the opposite hill. And yet it was part of his plan that the man should be following them. Looking back he could see no movement in the trees of the plantation but away to his right he noticed a covey of birds, ptarmigan, he thought, suddenly swirl up from the ground. Birds did not get up in

142

that way unless they had been frightened and he guessed that it must be the man with the rifle who had roused them. That would mean he was following and was making a detour around the plantation to avoid being slowed down by fighting his way through it.

When he had almost reached the crest of the ridge, he heard the report of the rifle. Instinctively he flinched and ducked but heard no bullet. Looking towards Katriona he saw that she was still on her feet, scrambling over a rocky shoulder just below the ridge. The sound of the shot was still echoing in the mountains around them when the man fired again, but once more there was no sound of a bullet thudding into the ground or ricocheting off a rock. Then he had reached safety and was careering breathlessly down the first few yards of the slope on the far side of the ridge.

When he joined Katriona she said, 'I thought you said we were out of range of that rifle.'

'We were, but either the man who fired it didn't realize that or he was just keeping the pressure on, trying to frighten us into doing something stupid.'

When he looked at the descent which faced them, Sanderson's relief at reaching the ridge safely was shattered. The other side of the mountain was bare, devoid of cover except for outcrops of rock and dangerously steep and he realized that he must have mistaken it for another mountain. His knowledge of that part of the Highlands was slight, gathered on a few days of hill walking and a little rock climbing, mostly done when he was a student and he knew now that he should not have trusted to his memory. Katriona and he would be able to get down the mountain but only with care, avoiding a sheer face of black rock to their left. Running and scrambling up the steep slopes to the ridge had, after the long walk to the bothy, left him physically drained, and Katriona must be on the point of exhaustion. So the descent would be slow, and if the man with the rifle were following them he would be at the ridge within minutes and have them in range and in full view. Sanderson saw, too, that going down that side of the mountain would not bring them, as he had expected, to a point near where they had left his car, but on to the main road from Glen Shiel at least two miles away.

The situation seemed hopeless. He ran back to the crest of the ridge and looked cautiously through a gap between two rocks down the slope which they had just climbed. The man was less than 200 yards away; a short, broad figure in knickerbockers and a sweater, moving swiftly even though he was impeded by the rifle he was carrying and the glasses slung round his neck. But Sanderson saw something else which brought at least a glimmer of hope. A huge, grey cloud was rolling in towards them from the other side of the glen. Much lower than the clouds they had seen sitting on top of the mountain peaks when they were driving down Glen Shiel earlier in the day, it seemed to fill the whole glen with a ghostly vapour as thick as any fog.

As he ran back to Katriona he looked at the terrain around them. To their left, nearer the summit of the mountain, was a large outcrop of rock, thick enough and uneven enough to provide a hiding place.

'Come on!' he shouted to Katriona. 'We'll make for those rocks.'

When they reached the rocks they clambered over them and dropped down panting on the grass the other side. Lying full length they would not be seen by the man with the rifle when he came over the ridge.

'Keep your head down,' Sanderson said. 'That red hair of yours will be like a beacon against this background.'

'Thanks very much! How long do we stay here?'

'The man with the rifle is coming up the other side. He'll be on the ridge in a few seconds.'

'And you think that if he doesn't see us he'll just go away?'

He motioned her to stop talking, for it would take too long to explain what he was relying on to save them. They lay quietly, not moving for a couple of minutes. They could hear nothing, which was reassuring for it meant that the man with the rifle must be some distance away, far enough at least not to stumble on them by accident. Cautiously and very slowly Sanderson raised his head till he could peer over the top of the rocks in front of them.

The man with the rifle was standing on the ridge. He had put the rifle down in the grass and was using his binoculars to make a slow sweep of the mountain slope below him. In only seconds he must know that the quarry he was hunting had not set off on a descent and that they must be hiding on or just over the ridge. Then he could begin to look around him for a hiding place and the rocks behind which they were lying was virtually the only one.

144

Sanderson ducked down again. What possible defence was there, he wondered, against a man armed with a rifle? A stone thrown quickly might catch the man off guard and if it flew true enough to strike him in the face or on the head, might stun him long enough to give them a chance. Frantically he looked around him for a stone of the right size.

Then, even as he had almost given up hope, he sensed a sudden dampness in the air. Thin wisps of mist floated in above the rocks as the cloud, cold and clammy, began to sweep over the ridge and down the other side of the mountain. It moved with astonishing speed and in seconds they were enveloped in a thick, swirling vapour that seemed to roll over them, blotting out the mountain peak, the slopes and even the rocks in front of them.

With visibility down to not more than ten or fifteen yards they were safe now from the man with the rifle, unless he literally bumped into them. Sanderson knew that they must begin making their way down the mountain towards the road. He beckoned to Katriona and moving as quietly as they could, they set off down the slope.

The descent in itself was hazardous enough. Remembering the rock face he had seen, Sanderson kept well to the right of the summit, afraid that in the mist they might stumble over the edge of a sheer drop of at least 200 feet. The mist played tricks with their vision and several times he saw what he took to be the figure of a man only for the shape to dissolve into a quite ordinary boulder as they drew nearer. Once the shadowy figure moved and they heard the sound of a stone slipping. They stopped walking at once and stood very still. The figure moved towards them and then they saw it was a solitary red deer which stared at them in astonishment and then turned to gallop away into the mist.

In parts the side of the mountain was too steep for walking and they had to slither down, always peering ahead for a hidden drop. Sanderson felt that he should be helping Katriona, but was afraid that she might resent any offer of help, reading it as a suggestion that women were weaker or less competent than men. He was conscious all the time that somewhere behind them was the man with the rifle, feeling his way through the mist, always listening for the noise that would betray them and waiting for the cloud to lift as suddenly as it had rolled in.

Then without warning they came out of the mist below the bottom of the cloud and could see the road below them. They had one final obstacle to negotiate; a burn swollen with the recent rain and tumbling down through rocks which they must cross. Sanderson crossed it first, leaping from one flat rock to another and then reached back instinctively to help Katriona. He thought at first she was going to refuse his hand but she took it, let him help her across and then said simply, 'Thanks'.

The final slope of the mountain was gentle enough for them to be able to run and presently they were sheltering behind a line of trees by the roadside. Looking back, Sanderson could see no sign of the man with the rifle and decided that he had either given up the chase or got lost in the mist. He grinned at Katriona as much with relief as elation.

'How do we get back to the car?' she asked.

'We wait for transport.'

Before long the transport arrived in the form of a battered Land Rover. Realizing that it must belong to a local farmer and not a tourist, Sanderson hailed it confidently. Highlanders were a courteous and kindly folk, always ready, in a region where distances were great, the roads lonely and the weather unpredictable, to give a lift to a stranded traveller.

He was right. The driver of the Land Rover stopped, picked them up and drove them down the road right up to Sanderson's Mercedes. Within a few seconds they were speeding towards the east, heading inland up Glen Shiel.

'Do you think we've shaken him off?' Katriona asked.

Sanderson looked in his driving mirror. The road behind him was empty for as far as he could see. 'It looks like it,' he replied. 'I only need a couple of minutes' start and he'll never catch us.'

The Mercedes was the perfect car for fast driving along the A87 as it wound its way back up Glen Shiel. With no hedges or dry stone walls to impede his view, Sanderson could see the road ahead for a full half-mile or more and even at 90 the car would hold the road without skidding on all but the sharpest bends. There was little traffic, no tour buses labouring up the hills, no tiny family cars crawling like beetles as their bespectacled middle-aged occupants admired the uninspiring waters of Loch Shiel. On the rare occasions when they had to overtake a slower vehicle, the Mercedes, with its narrow wheelbase and the extra acceleration at its command, swept past with contemptuous ease.

In a short time they took the sharp right-hand turn to cross the river and began to climb again, heading south towards Invergarry. Only then did Katriona seem to relax and Sanderson could sense her relief. She repeated the question she had asked earlier.

'Who on earth could have fired those shots at us?'

'I can't begin even to guess. Did you tell anyone we were coming up here today?'

'No one,' she replied, and then immediately added, 'No. That's not strictly true.'

'What do you mean?'

'My mother 'phoned yesterday to ask if I would go over to see her today. She wants to talk about my father's will. I told her I know nothing about a will or even whether he left one, but she pressed me to go. She and Jock are growing restless.'

'Then she must be hoping your father has left her money.'

'I wouldn't think so, but if he has left me any she'll be looking for a loan. Anyway I was weak. I said I'd go for lunch today. Then after you rang last night I left a note for Gillian asking if she would call my mother and explain that I had changed my plans and was driving up to Wester Ross with you.'

'Is that all you said? You didn't tell her where we were coming and why?'

'How could I? I didn't know myself until we set out.'

Sanderson looked in his driving mirror. If Katriona had told no one of the bothy in which he had met her father and the purpose of their journey there that day, it could only mean that he had been followed all the way north. And yet he had not at any time been aware of having anyone on his tail. Like many people who had learnt to drive on the narrow roads in the wilder parts of Scotland, he used his driving mirror a good deal and he liked to think he was observant. If a car of the same make and colour had been reflected in the mirror for any length of time he would surely have noticed it.

At all events he was reasonably satisfied that they were not being followed now. But as a precaution he continued to drive as fast as he safely could and soon they came to the junction with the main trunk road from Inverness to Glasgow. There was traffic heading south and he managed to slip neatly in between a lorry carrying milk churns and one of the huge continental juggernauts which, with the protection of the lunatic Common Market regulations, were rapidly destroying Scotland's roads. For no logical reason, having the monster behind him gave Sanderson an added sense of security as the small caravan of vehicles drove at a sedate pace towards the Great Glen.

Then, as they rounded a bend, almost without warning the caravan came to a halt. In front of the milk lorry red lights were flashing and Sanderson realized that they had been stopped short of the swing bridge by which the road crossed the Caledonian Canal before continuing along the east bank of Loch Lochy. He had driven along the road many times during his life without ever being stopped at the bridge. Now it was swung aside to allow two small vessels to pass up the canal.

The delay did not concern him overmuch, for he was certain that they had outwitted the sniper who had fired at them and were not being followed. Then as they waited, he glanced in his driving mirror once again and saw at the very end of the line of cars and lorries which stretched back behind them to a bend in the road, a brown Porsche.

He remembered the car that had been standing in the car park by the Cluanie Inn just as he and Katriona were leaving after their lunch. That had been a brown Porsche. A rather drab shade of brown was not a colour which he associated with Porsches, whose owners in his experience preferred brighter, more conspicuous hues; red, black and bright-green. The thought struck him that brown was a colour one might choose if one did not wish one's car to be noticed. But the Porsche behind them might not be the same car as the one they had seen by the Cluanie Inn, and even if it were that need not have any sinister significance. The driver of the Porsche might easily have motored up to Wester Ross for the afternoon to visit friends or just for the drive and now be returning home.

When the bridge had been swung back into position, the line of waiting vehicles moved off. As soon as he had the chance, Sanderson overtook the milk lorry. To come up behind him the Porsche, he knew, would have to pass several cars, not to mention the juggernaut, on a road which, with its many bends and overhanging trees, was not made

148

for fast driving. A plan had already formed in his mind. With nothing in front to hold him up, he would pull away and be out of sight of the Porsche before they reached Spean Bridge. There he would turn off the main road and drive up over the moors to join the A9 at Dalwhinnie and then head south. If the driver of the Porsche had followed them all the way from Glasgow, he would be expecting them to return by the same route and would not think of turning off at Spean Bridge but keep straight on, knowing that he would be able to catch them up when they were slowed down by having to pass through Fort William. It was a precaution, nothing more, for he was still far from convinced that they were being followed.

As they drove along by Loch Lochy, he sensed that some of Katriona's tenseness had returned. She had never once looked round so she could not have seen the brown Porsche and he wondered whether she had in some way been infected by his own anxiety. He tried to reopen a conversation, but she replied to his small talk with only the briefest remarks.

Then suddenly, glancing at his mirror, he saw the Porsche again. It was two or three hundred yards behind, tucked in behind a red Ford. To have escaped from the caravan of vehicles and passed the juggernaut it must have been driven not only fast but recklessly. He slowed down and the Ford drew nearer but the Porsche seemed to hold back. Scrapping his first plan he decided on another.

'Shall we stop for a drink?' he asked Katriona.

'Will the pubs be open yet? It's Sunday, remember.'

'They will be opening in a few minutes.'

They swung round a left-hand bend and he saw in front of them the entrance of Letterfinlay Lodge hotel. Sanderson knew the place, for he had stopped there more than once for a meal or a drink. The hotel stood in attractive grounds on the edge of the loch and the drive which led up to it formed a fork with the main road not far in front of them and to their right. He scarcely had to slow down at all as he swung the Mercedes into it, nor did he indicate that he was turning. The driver of the Ford gave a short blast on his horn to show his disapproval of this poor roadmanship but drove on past the entrance towards Spean Bridge and so did the brown Porsche.

It was only when they were sitting in the bar with drinks in front of

149

them that Katriona said, 'We're being followed, aren't we?'

'Possibly. I can't be sure.'

She seemed displeased. 'Bruce, you don't have to protect me, you know.'

He told her about the Porsche and explained why he had suggested stopping for a drink and then added, 'We'll soon know if I am right.'

'What do you suppose the driver will do now if he was following us?'

'Wait hidden in the trees just up the road somewhere until we go past and then get back on our tail.'

'And if he does, what then?'

'I don't know. We'll have to play it off the cuff.'

'Was there one person in the Porsche or two?' Katriona asked.

'I only saw one man.'

'In that case would we not be safe so long as we kept in the car? One can scarcely drive a fast car and fire a rifle at the same time. And surely he wouldn't shoot at us on the open road with other traffic about.'

'Whatever route we take driving home, we'll have to cover some long stretches of empty road.' Sanderson was thinking of the country beyond Glencoe, with its lonely moors and silent lochs, deserted even in the peak of the tourist season except for an occasional car or caravan. 'And it will be dark before long. That character in the Porsche could easily force us off the road whenever he liked up there and kill us at his leisure. A man who was ready to fire at us in the glen might do almost anything.'

'I told you that I didn't need protecting,' Katriona said and smiled. 'That doesn't mean you have to frighten the life out of me.'

Sanderson wondered whether she was as unconcerned as she appeared to be or whether her flippancy was no more than a brave façade. The events of the afternoon had at first seemed totally unreal and it was only now that he realized the danger he was facing. He had blundered into a situation which was no concern of his, like a careless hiker straying into a gunnery range. Violence was exploding about him and all at once he was the target. If Katriona showed no signs of fear, did that mean she was concealing it or that she knew she was not in danger?

After finishing their drinks they left the hotel, rejoined the main road and drove south past Spean Bridge, Glenlochy distillery and into Fort William. It was only as they were leaving the town, passing the row of tourist hotels which stood facing Loch Linnhe across the road that they saw the Porsche again. Sanderson could not be certain but it appeared to come out of the centre of the town, where perhaps the driver had been waiting for them and joined the main road at the roundabout, before slipping in at a comfortable distance behind the Mercedes.

'Don't look round,' he told Katriona, 'but our friend in the Porsche is behind us.'

'Why should I not look?'

'If he believes we don't suspect that we're being followed, it will be easier to give him the slip.'

The new plan he had conceived for shaking off the Porsche depended on his knowledge of the countryside which had been his home for many years, but even so it would need luck to succeed. He drove steadily for half a dozen miles or so, never exceeding 50, which was a perfectly normal speed for the twisting road and then, a mile or so short of Corran, he had his first stroke of luck as they caught up with a coachload of trippers from Newcastle. To capitalize on the luck he took a chance with a piece of driving reckless to the point of lunacy, overtaking the coach with a sudden burst of speed right at the beginning of a sharp bend and only just squeezing past an oncoming car, whose driver flashed his lights and hooted in alarm.

The first bend was followed by others as he knew it would be and by taking them as fast as he dared, with screeching tyres, he came out of the last of them with the Porsche well back out of sight. Almost immediately they were at the slip road which led to the Corran ferry and he swung into it at speed. As he well remembered, it sloped sharply down to the jetty from which the ferry sailed so that in seconds the Mercedes would be out of view from the main road.

When he reached the line of vehicles which stood waiting for the ferry and took his place behind them, he saw that luck was still with him. The squat, rectangular shape of the ferry could be seen midway in the straights and it was coming towards them. In a few minutes it would reach the ramp and in another ten it would have discharged its cargo of vehicles, loaded up again and be setting off for the opposite shore of Ardgour.

Katriona looked over her shoulder. 'You seem to have shaken our friend off,' she said.

151

'We'll see. When he finds we're no longer in front of him he may well guess what we've done. If our luck holds though, we may be on the ferry and away before he comes back.'

'And where does the ferry take us?'

'To Ardgour, and from there we'll drive to Ardnamurchan where I lived when I was a lad.'

While they waited, Sanderson looked down the line of vehicles which stretched before them to the loading ramp of the ferry. At the front of the line was a van, painted white but stained with mud and dirt, which bore the name of a hotel in Ardnamurchan, The Highland Welcome Hotel. Fifteen years previously the hotel had been owned by the father of one of his boyhood friends, Neil Adamson. He remembered the days he had spent in and around the hotel, lingering with Neil when they were children in a corner of the bar listening to the talk of the visitors, later when they were older waiting at table in the dining-room and being rewarded by Neil's father with a few shillings or, in defiance of the law, with a pint of heavy.

Putting reverie and nostalgia out of his mind, he looked behind him. Two more cars had arrived and taken their places behind them. Two or three more and there would be as many as the ferry could hold. If the Porsche then arrived, it would have to wait for the next crossing and he and Katriona would be across the straights and in Ardnamurchan where he knew they would be safe. The ferry wallowed in, lowered its metal bows on to the concrete ramp and the vehicles it had brought over began disembarking, obeying the instructions of the two lads who made up the vessel's crew. The last car was off and the lads were signalling to the white van at the front of the waiting line to drive up the ramp, when the Porsche appeared, swinging down the incline from the main road, hesitating for a moment and then joining the end of the queue.

## 17

KATRIONA SAT ALONE in the Mercedes as the ferry nosed its way towards the white lighthouse on the far shore of the loch. It had to sail crabwise, its bows pointed well off course to counteract the drift of a powerful current. Loch Linnhe, she had been told, was tidal and in a high wind the tide-race could be fierce enough to give the ferry a rough passage. Before the war the old ferry had been known to sink on more than one occasion.

Bruce had left the car and gone forward to a shabby white van which stood in the row of vehicles nearest to the bows of the ferry. He had recognized the driver, he had told her, as a friend of his boyhood and now they were deep in conversation through the open window of the van. Men, Katriona knew, when they met a friend of their school-days, even after many years of separation, were able instantly to rekindle the spirit of their former friendship and start an orgy of reminiscences which delighted them but from which any women present were automatically excluded. It was a habit that had often irritated her. As the ferry approached the far shore, he returned to the Mercedes but said nothing about his friend or their conversation, and that too irritated Katriona, although she recognized that there was no reason why she should expect him to talk to her about his private life.

When they left the ferry, Bruce turned westwards along the broad new highway. The day was fading but there was still light enough to give a splendid view across Loch Linnhe of Beinn Bheithir and Bidean nam Bian, both well above 3,000 feet, standing guard, it seemed, above Ballachulish and the village of Glencoe. The white van was in front of them and Bruce made no attempt to overtake it, holding his place between it and another car behind. Katriona did not look round but she guessed that the Porsche would not be far away and she was right.

They drove for several miles along the new road, with open moorland to the south and Garbh Bheinn to the north, until they could see the head of Loch Sunart in front of them. Then without warning the road changed, the highway giving way abruptly to a narrow strip of tarred surface; one of those roads still typical of the West Highlands, too narrow to allow even the smallest of cars to pass or overtake, so that every 200 yards or so they are cut back a few feet to make passing places which are marked by white posts.

Bruce stayed behind the hotel van which was forced to reduce its speed to negotiate the bends in the road and its sharp rises and falls as it followed the contours of the small bays and coves which formed the shore of the loch. Almost at once they were passing through the little village of Strontian standing above a small beach ringed with trees, on which a few boats lay forlornly. If anything, the road beyond the village seemed to grow even narrower, threading its way through woodland and escaping from the oaks and larches every now and then to provide a view of the still waters of the loch reflecting the last of the evening light.

Bruce was following close behind the van, too close it seemed to Katriona, and they both pulled away a little from the car immediately to their rear. Then, as they were approaching a passing place, the van pulled into it, the driver waving them to overtake him before he cut back quickly on to the road again. As soon as they were past the van, Bruce accelerated and the Mercedes leapt forward with a surge of power.

'Hold on to your hats!' he called out grinning.

'Bruce! Are you mad? What are you doing?'

'We're going to fix that bastard in the Porsche. No one can overtake on this road unless the car in front allows him to. My friend Neil will hold him back while we get away. In a few minutes we'll be out of his sight and he'll not find us, I promise you.'

'Unless you kill us both before.'

'Don't fash yourself. I was driving on these roads when I was fourteen.'

His confidence did little to reassure Katriona. She was not in the normal way a nervous passenger in a car, but Bruce was throwing the Mercedes round every bend and down every slope with a reckless

154

abandon which made it appear inevitable that they would either slither into the woods or hit the mossy stone wall which ran alongside the loch. After passing the village of Salen they had a choice of roads, a rare luxury in Ardnamurchan, and Bruce took the one leading to the west.

A mile or two further on, after they had skidded round a right-hand bend, turning inland away from the loch, swerved past a rocky outcrop which crowded the road and slipped through a narrow arch of over-hanging trees, Bruce braked suddenly and almost as violently as he had accelerated a few minutes earlier. To their left Katriona saw an open gate in a wire fence and a short driveway which dropped steeply down to a bungalow, one of half a dozen which had been built in a copse between the road and loch. With a quick flick of the steering wheel, Bruce swung the car through the gate and down the drive. A small wooden shed which served as a garage stood beside the bungalow.

'Quick! Open the garage doors. They're not locked,' he told Katriona.

She left the car and did as he had asked. When the Mercedes was safely in the shed and the engine switched off, he came out and closed the doors, took a bunch of keys from his pocket and let them into the house. Once they were both inside he stood by the front door listening, but there was nothing to be heard; not the sound of a car engine nor voices nor footsteps, nothing except the wind in the trees and from the loch behind them the plaintive cries of sea birds.

'What do we do now?' Katriona asked.

'We wait for my friend Neil. He has promised to come round as soon as he can with food and anything else we might need for the night.'

Suspicion, which always seemed to be lying dormant beneath Katriona's reserve, emerged, sharp and alert. 'You're not suggesting that we spend the night here?'

'We've no alternative. There's only one road back to the mainland and our friend in the Porsche will be watching that, you can be sure.'

'When did you arrange this?'

'When I spoke to Neil on the ferry coming over. He'll work out a plan for getting us away in the morning.'

His answer did not satisfy her and she seemed to brood over it for a time. They went into the living-room of the bungalow which

155

overlooked the loch. Dusk had turned suddenly into darkness and Bruce drew the curtains and switched on the lights. The bungalow was the holiday home of a family from Kelso, which they let out when they were not using it themselves. Neil, now the proprietor of his late father's hotel, held the keys for them in between lets and kept an eye on the property generally. But the owner of the Porsche would not know that and no one in Ardnamurchan except Neil would know where he had hidden Katriona and Bruce.

'Are you sure we were being followed?' Katriona asked, and there was a coldness in the question.

'Absolutely certain. Aren't you?'

'You forget that I never actually saw this Porsche.'

Only slowly did Bruce understand the implication of her remark and the reason for her suspicion. When he had overcome his incredulity he wanted to laugh. He said, 'You believe I planned all this in advance, don't you? That it was a way of tricking you into spending a night alone with me in this house?'

'It had struck me that might be your motive,' she replied coldly, but Bruce noticed that she had the decency to blush.

'Katriona,' Bruce began, wondering how he should phrase what he wished to say so that it would sound tactful. 'You've never once done anything or said anything which would lead me to believe that you had any kind of personal interest in me, have you?'

'No.'

'Then how could I have possibly imagined that you would be willing to sleep with me?'

'Men are capable of believing anything.'

'Let me put it another way then,' Bruce said patiently. 'You're an attractive girl. I admit that. But have I ever done or said anything to suggest that I might wish to sleep with you?'

Anger flared in her eyes. 'There is no need for you to be offensive.'

They had reached an impasse. Neither tact nor patience, Bruce decided, would ever prevail against the spiky defences of a girl who appeared to take a perverse pleasure in finding an insult in every remark. Leaving her in the living-room, he went into the kitchen of the bungalow to forage. The tension of the past few hours had left him in need of a drink. But the last people to have rented the house had been good Scots, tidy as well as thrifty. They had left nothing, no whisky, no cans of beer, not even a spoonful of tea.

When he returned to the living-room, Katrina still looked hurt and angry. 'I'm sorry that I got you into this fix,' he told her. 'It was wrong of me to take you up to the bothy.'

'That's all right.'

'It's not all right. I should have realized that I would be putting you in some danger.'

'How could you possibly have known that?' The tone of her question showed that she still was not convinced that there had been any danger.

'Simon, a friend of mine, was attacked and killed on Friday night outside the flat where I'm staying. Did you not read about it in the papers?'

'No.'

Bruce realized now as he thought about it that Katriona was not likely to have read of Simon's death. It had happened too late at night to catch the morning papers the following day and she would have left Edinburgh too early to see the Sunday papers. 'We thought at first that Simon had been set upon by some roughs he had met in a pub,' he told her. 'Simon went drinking in strange places. Now I'm certain he was attacked by mistake. He was mistaken for me.'

Katriona looked at him, still sceptical as he told her about the circumstances of the attack on Simon. He explained that he had been killed by a single blow.

'Why didn't you tell me this before?' she asked.

'I wasn't sure that it was connected in any way with your father's murder. After what happened this afternoon I know it was.'

'Do you really believe that they meant to kill you?'

'Not on Friday night. If they had they would have come round with something more lethal than a whisky bottle. No, I think that was meant to frighten me off. They would have known I had been to your father's house and up to the distilleries he had visited the day before he disappeared. They must have thought I was getting too near the truth.'

'And this afternoon?'

'The man on the hill must have been watching us with binoculars.

He would have seen that we had found something in the bothy.'

'Something important enough for him to kill us so that he could get hold of it?'

'Apparently so.'

'I suppose you still have the papers and the tape.'

In the confusion which had followed the first rifle shot, Bruce had forgotten about the papers and the cassette. He remembered now that he had put them in his hip pocket. They were still there. He took the sheets of paper out and unfolded them. At the bothy they had read only the first of the three sheets. Now, looking at the second and the third, they found MacNair's notes on the launching of his new product The Spirit of Scotland. This was to be done with an advertising campaign, mainly in the wine and spirit trade journals but also with poster advertising and a special introductory price discount offer. MacNair had been confident that the largest supermarket chain in Scotland would co-operate in the launching, which would be timed to coincide with a major food and drink exhibition in Glasgow where the Loch Rannoch Whisky Company would have a stand to display the new drink. This would be followed by a whole series of different promotions, some of them ambitious and costly, including the sponsorship of a pageant of Scottish history under the title of The Spirit of Scotland at the next Edinburgh Festival.

When it came to how the launch and promotion were to be financed, MacNair's notes were much less informative. They only referred to a bank loan and hinted that negotiations had already been started with the Strathclyde Linen Bank.

When they had finished reading the two sheets, Katriona remarked, 'In his letter to me my father mentioned an exciting new project which he would explain to me when he came to dinner. This must be it.'

'Yes. He spoke of it to me as well, without giving any details. He must have been afraid that someone was trying to steal the secret.'

'Can it be so important?'

'I find it hard to see how it could be, but if it isn't how do you explain that someone tried to kill us to get hold of these?' Bruce held up the sheets.

'Unless it's the cassette that they are after. I wonder what's on the tape.'

'We can't find out until we get home,' Bruce replied. 'There won't be a microcassette recorder on the whole of Ardnamurchan, for sure.'

'What's on the other side of the sheets of paper?'

Turning one of the sheets over, they saw that it was a type of standard printed form, a delivery order on to which various details had been typed. The other two sheets were the same. They stared at one of the sheets together.

THE BONNIE BRAES WHISKY CORP.

Madison Avenue,

New York 10010

*DELIVERY ORDER*

Acc. No. 1463       Inv. 2710       July 12, 1973.

To: The Warehouse Keeper,
      Glen Cromach Distillery,
      By Tomintoul,
      Banffshire.

Please deliver the undermentioned goods to the order of:-
      J. S. Gannon, jnr.
      623 Indian Creek Avenue,
      Tampa, Florida.

| *Cask* | *Whisky* | *Bonded date* | *Cask Nos.* |
|---|---|---|---|
| 5, Hogsheads | Glen Cromach Malt | 1972 | 8501–8505. |

C

O

P

Y

*New Owner:-* J. S. Gannon, jnr.

The Bonnie Braes Whisky Corp.

by:- P. Lawson.

The other two pages of MacNair's notes had also been written on the backs of delivery orders, identical except for the names of the new owners of the whisky, both of whom had addresses in other parts of America. In every case the amount of whisky transferred was five hogsheads. All three forms were discoloured at the edges with age.

Looking at them and noticing the dates on which they had been filled in, Bruce remembered Mrs Hastie telling him of how MacNair had decided to streamline the files and records of the Loch Rannoch Whisky Company and in so doing threw away large quantities of old documents and papers.

'Do you suppose these forms could have any significance?' Katriona asked him.

'I wouldn't think so. Look at the dates on them. My guess is that they were part of a bundle of documents that was to be junked and that your father simply started to use them instead of scrap paper.'

They did not have to wait long for Neil. Presently they heard a gentle tapping on the window of the living-room which overlooked the loch. Bruce let him through the back door which led off the kitchen. He was not at all Katriona's idea of a hotelier, with neither any artificial politeness nor a trace of obsequiousness. Thickset and comfortably overweight, he was dressed in a sweater and a scruffy pair of jeans and had the ruddy complexion and very pale eyes of one who spent much of his life looking into distant spaces, in search of a stag, perhaps, or a covey of birds. He was carrying a haversack which he set down on a table and unpacked.

'Chicken drumsticks, Arbroath smokie pâté, pork pie,' he intoned solemnly as he laid out each of the provisions he had brought. 'Dundee cake, Caboc cheese, baps, oatcakes, a flask of tea. And whisky, of course.'

'That's great. I'm starving!' Bruce exclaimed.

'Sorry it's not something grander.' Neil glanced shyly at Katriona. 'Sheena could not understand why the pair of you were not coming to take your supper with us.'

'You're very kind to go to such trouble.'

'I'm sorry, too, that I've been so long in coming. I cut back from the hotel through the woods and down on to the loch shore a wee way along in case your man was watching.' He grinned at Bruce. 'Nice friends you've picked up in the south, Bruce!'

'What happened?'

'Yon character in the Porsche blasted me off the road.'

'Blasted?'

'Aye, literally.'

160

Neil told them how after Bruce had overtaken his van he continued along the narrow twisting road, followed by the other car which had come off the ferry and behind that the Porsche. After a minute or two the other car had pulled into a passing place to let the Porsche overtake.

'He came up behind me, hooting and flashing his lights to show he wanted to pass,' Neil said, 'but I ignored him. Then suddenly I heard an explosion and immediately I lost control of the van. Next thing I knew I was down the bank into the trees. I thought at first that I'd had a blow-out, but when I looked at the nearside back wheel it was no longer there, only a splintered hub. Your pal in the Porsche had blown it right off with some kind of hand-gun, I suppose.'

'Christ, I'm sorry Neil!' Bruce exclaimed. 'The man must be a nutter.'

'We'll pay for the damage, of course,' Katriona said at once.

'Let's see what the insurance company has to say. Perhaps they'll see it as an act of God,' Neil replied, and then he added, 'The first priority is to work out how we can get you away safely.'

Neil's plan for getting them away from Ardnamurchan was ingenious. He and his wife would come to the bungalow at first light the next morning, fetch Bruce's car and drive it to the Corran ferry. The driver of the Porsche, he was confident, would be watching the road to the ferry and would follow them, thinking they were Bruce and Katriona. Soon afterwards a van from the local grocer's store would call at the bungalow, ostensibly to deliver an order. Bruce and Katriona would be smuggled into the van and driven to Kilchoan at the other end of the Ardnamurchan peninsula, where they would catch the passenger ferry to Tobermory on Mull, and from Mull another ferry to Oban.

'We'll not allow you to do this, Neil,' Bruce protested. 'God knows what that character would do when he found out it was you and Sheena in my car.'

'We'll have an escort,' Neil replied. 'It's all arranged. Sandy will follow us all the way to the ferry. You remember Sandy Tait, of course? He's with the police now.'

One last precaution had been built into Neil's plan. If the Porsche followed the Mercedes to the ferry and took its place in the line of cars waiting to board, Sandy and his colleague in the police car would approach it on some pretext or other, asking to see the driver's licence and delaying him long enough so that he could not catch the same ferry as Neil. Having crossed the straits, Neil and Sheena would drive down to Oban where they would meet up with Katriona and Bruce, returning later to Ardnamurchan by way of Mull.

'How much have you told Sandy?' Bruce asked Neil.

'Nothing. It's better that he doesn't know how dangerous this man in the Porsche is. And you know Sandy. He'll guess something is wrong but he won't ask.'

'We're putting you to a deal of trouble,' Katriona remarked.

'We're enjoying it. It'll be a day out for Sheena and me. There's not much excitement on Ardnamurchan, as you've probably realized.'

The three of them discussed the details of the plan for a little longer and then Neil left, slipping out of the back door of the bungalow into the darkness. When they were alone Katriona and Bruce ate the food which he had brought them, hungrily, for they had burnt up a good deal of energy, nervous as well as physical, in a long afternoon. They ate silently, exchanging no more than a word or two and then when they had finished Bruce poured them both a second glass of whisky.

As they sat on the sofa drinking she said suddenly and abruptly, 'I apologize for my behaviour earlier on.'

'No need for apologies at all.'

'I'm sorry I doubted you. The trouble is, Bruce, that I don't trust people any more. No, let's be more specific. I no longer trust men.'

Bruce knew from the way she was speaking that apologies did not come easily to her. He said, 'When a girl says that it usually means she has been badly hurt.'

Even as he made it Bruce felt slightly ashamed of the remark, a trite observation, tossed off unthinkingly because their conversation did not really interest him, but Katriona looked at him in surprise and asked, 'How did you know?'

'How did I know what?'

'While I was at university I met a man named Tom Robertson. He failed his course and was sent down after two years. After I had graduated I lived with him for six years. Tom was intelligent enough

162

but he couldn't keep a job. He was full of bright schemes and all of them failed. Perhaps I felt sorry for him. Anyway I kept him for six years; paid for everything, his clothes, his holidays, his whisky. I lent him money to start a business, a small chain of launderettes, but that was a disaster and so was his next venture, a travel agency. I recognized his failings all right but I came to believe he would not be able to manage without me.'

'But he could?'

'Tom borrowed money from me, saying he wanted to go to Spain, where he had a chance of becoming a partner in a company selling villas to the English. He came back six weeks later, just to collect his things, you'll understand. He had moved in with a girl he had met in London and said he was thinking of marrying her.'

'Nice guy!'

'He went to some trouble to tell me how boring I was and how lousy he had always found me in bed.'

Her hand shook as she lifted her glass to her lips and a little whisky spilt on to her tweed slacks. She had not been looking at him as she was speaking but staring straight in front of her across the room. Bruce wondered whether the whisky was starting to affect her, but decided that a girl who had shared a full bottle of claret and followed it with a Benedictine as Katriona had when they dined together, would not become fou after a couple of drams.

Turning her head, she looked at him. 'You've no idea how shattering it is,' she said in a small, tight voice, 'to be rejected.'

'Are you forgetting? I was thrown out of my job.'

She made no reply. Instead her mouth trembled like a small child's might after a rebuke or a disappointment. He saw then that there were tears in her eyes and presently they spilled out. She cried soundlessly, no sobs, just a steady course of tears down her cheeks.

'Kate, don't!' he said, and reached out to touch her hand.

'No!' She pulled away. 'Don't try to comfort me! Like all men you'll be despising a woman's weakness.'

'Weakness! My God, Kate, do you realize what you've been through today? The danger you've been in? We could both easily be dead!'

'You've faced it too.'

'Yes and most of the time I was scared to hell.'

This time when he reached out to take her hands she did not pull

163

them away. It was only when he was holding them that he noticed the scratches and grazes and bruises which covered them; scratches from forcing her way through closely planted trees, grazes and bruises from the rocks and boulders over which they had scrambled. She had never once complained or even exclaimed aloud in pain.

He raised her hands to his lips. As soon as he had kissed them he regretted it. Sentiment was totally out of keeping with his character and it was the kind of gesture calculated to inflame Katriona's defensive resentment and provoke a stinging comment.

Her response was equally out of character. She smiled at him through her tears and leant back against the sofa. Nor did she protest when he put his arm around her shoulders. Presently the tears stopped and she closed her eyes.

A few moments later, when he realized she was asleep, he went into one of the bedrooms and came back with a blanket to lay over her.

## 18

As Katriona and Bruce crossed on the ferry from Craignure to Oban, the weather began to clear. In the morning a haar had hung over Ardnamurchan, enveloping the road that ran along the edge of the loch and the moors which it crossed when it turned inland towards Kilchoan. At Tobermory a friend of Neil had been waiting for them when they left the passenger ferry and he had driven them to Craignure. Now they stood on the deck of the vessel looking over the rail, not towards Oban but at the receding coast of Mull.

'What do we do when we reach Oban?' Katriona asked.

'Drive to your father's house and play that cassette back. It may tell us what we want to know.'

'Do you not think we should tell the police in Oban about what happened yesterday?'

'What do we tell them? That someone took pot shots at us up in the hills and that a man in a Porsche followed us south? Even if they believed us what could they do? No, the only way we're going to be safe is by finding out what the hell this is all about.'

Neil and his wife were waiting for them on the quay at Oban and the Mercedes was parked unobtrusively in a street behind one of the hotels that stood facing the sea. Sheena was a small, shy woman with blue eyes and dark hair, the daughter of a farmer from Lochaber who had studied cooking in London and was agreed to be the finest cook within 50 miles of their hotel.

'Did our friend in the Porsche appear?' Bruce asked them.

'Yes. He came out of nowhere and followed us all the way to Ardgour,' Sheena replied.

'But you shook him off?'

'Yes. At least Sandy did. We were in line waiting for the ferry when up came the police car and Sandy went over to the driver of the

Porsche. We boarded the ferry and they were still arguing as it pulled out into the loch.'

When they reached the Mercedes Bruce asked Neil what he and Sheena would do with the rest of the day. Neil replied, 'We had planned to go straight home by way of Mull but we've changed our minds. We'll take a bus to Fort William and try out someone else's cooking for a change. Then Morag, who works in the hotel, is driving out after lunch to pick us up.'

'Thank you for everything,' Katriona said and when Neil went to shake her hand, she leaned forward unexpectedly and kissed him on the cheek. 'I don't know how we can ever repay you.'

'It was nothing.'

'You risked your lives for us.'

'Och, away with you!'

'Now you come and see us soon,' Sheena said. 'The pair of you. Come for the day or a weekend if you can manage it.'

'We will.'

When they were driving away from Oban, Bruce thought about the way Sheena had invited them to visit Ardnamurchan, treating them as a couple, good friends if not something more. Did this mean, he wondered, that after the events of the last 24 hours he and Katriona had moved closer together and did this new intimacy show? Katriona had not seemed offended or embarrassed by the way Sheena had phrased her invitation.

Once or twice as they were driving along she glanced back over her shoulder. 'What are you looking for?' he teased her. 'A man in a Porsche?' And when she nodded he remarked, 'So you do believe we were being followed?'

'That's not fair! I did apologize.'

'Don't worry! Once he knows that he has lost us he'll scurry back home to hide. Either that or he'll be reporting to whoever sent him after us.'

They reached Bridge of Allan early in the afternoon and after crossing the river, turned up the hill towards MacNair's house. The streets were empty, the houses silent and seemingly asleep. They saw no one in the streets up on the hill except an elderly couple out for a walk, the man in a tweed suit and green deer stalker, the woman

166

holding on to his arm, one of the many retired couples who lived in Bridge of Allan, and out for a walk, not so much for exercise but to relieve the tedium of a long, empty day.

Leaving the Mercedes outside MacNair's house, Katriona and Bruce went straight to the study. The microcassette recorder was still lying on the desk where Bruce had seen it on his last visit to the house. He took the tiny cassette out of its plastic case, slipped it into place and switched on the machine. Ian MacNair's voice, even against a good deal of background noise and distorted with a metallic timbre, was instantly recognizable.

'My initial plan for the composition of the S.O.S. blend,' the recording began, 'allows for sixty-four per cent of grain whisky and thirty-six per cent malt whisky. Orders have already been placed for fillings of three different grain whiskies and I envisage using them in approximately equal proportions. I expect to be using twenty-two Highland malts, probably the following.'

The recording went on to list the various Highland malts which MacNair had planned to use and then the Lowland malts and Islay malts. After that it gave an estimate of the proportions of these malts which MacNair would use in his blend.

'I can't see how this information could be of such importance to anyone,' Katriona observed.

'Nor can I. Shall we skip a little of the tape? Maybe there's something more interesting to follow.'

Switching on the fast forward control button of the recorder, he ran it for a few seconds and began playing the tape from that point. MacNair was still giving technical details of how the Spirit of Scotland blend was to be produced, the amount of caramel which would have to be used to bring the spirit up to the colour of whisky and the size and shape of the bottles in which it would be sold. To make sure that it contained no other message, they ran the tape through to the end.

'That was not exactly helpful,' Bruce said. 'I for one am no wiser.'

'Why don't we listen to the other side?'

He did as Katriona suggested, ejecting the cassette and then replacing it in the machine to play the other side of the tape. Once again they heard MacNair's voice, but this time the tone was

167

perceptibly different, self-conscious, as though he were speaking for an audience.

'This is to identify myself. It is Iain MacNair of Bridge of Allan speaking and what I am about to say should be interpreted as my last will and testament.' A pause followed, as though MacNair had rehearsed the opening sentences, but was now not certain how he should continue. Presently he went on, 'Like many people, I had been intending to make a will but kept procrastinating, telling myself it could wait. A few days ago, however, an attempt was made to kill me. If my assumptions about this attempt on my life and about the people behind it are correct, then there is almost certain to be a second attempt. So I decided today, on the eve of leaving for a walking holiday in the West of Scotland, that I would record my wishes for the disposal of my property and personal effects in case I were to die before I have an opportunity of instructing my solicitor to draw up a proper will.'

Bruce glanced sideways at Katriona. She was listening intently to the recording and he wondered what emotions her father's words were arousing in her. Was it nothing more than curiosity or did she feel any remorse for the way she had treated her father? He did not discount the possibility that all she felt was expectation, believing that her father might have made her a legacy.

'In any event,' the message continued, 'a will is really no more than a formality, for I have only one natural heir, my daughter Katriona. It has been one of the sadnesses of my life that Katriona and I have been estranged for so long.' Now MacNair's diction and tone changed again, his words became clipped and his voice impersonal. A typically Scottish reaction, Bruce thought, a closing up, a determination not to give way to emotion. 'But the fault was as much mine as hers and my affection for her remains undiminished. What I did was considered to be in her best interests and I would like to hope that one day she will realize that and will understand.'

Knowing what he did about the relationship between father and daughter and that it had only been MacNair's murder which had prevented a reconciliation, Bruce found the words, stiff and clipped though they sounded, oddly poignant. He glanced at Katriona again but this time, as he did so, she looked away in order, he supposed, to hide her emotion.

'The provisions of my will are simple enough,' MacNair's voice continued. 'Katriona will not know but I used a substantial part of the money which I received when I left MacNair's Whisky Company to buy a stake in Peter Wandercliff's business. The shares were all bought in her name. In addition, since her mother and I separated I have been putting money into a trust created on Katriona's behalf, the trustees of which are Sir Douglass Tweedie and Peter Wandercliff. I also leave my home at Bridge of Allan to my daughter but I have decided to leave my other house in Drymen to my former wife, Brenda. She has lived there, happily I hope, for many years and I would like to think that it would continue to be her home. The only other bequests I have to make are of personal effects, mementos for my friends; my gold watch, cuff links and dress studs to Peter Wandercliff and my guns and fishing-rods to Douglass Tweedie. Finally, and an important point, I believe I have left sufficient funds in my personal bank accounts and in securities to meet any death duties payable on my estate.'

The message ended abruptly and Bruce had the impression that MacNair may have intended finishing what he had to say with a personal statement of some kind, but that he had been unable to find words to express his feelings. He said nothing as he switched off the recorder. To have made any comment at all might well have embarrassed Katriona and to congratulate her on her good fortune would be tactless. So he waited for her to speak.

'He has left me almost everything,' she said at last. 'I wish he hadn't.'

'Why not?'

'No one can say I deserve it. I treated him shamefully.'

'But you knew about the trust he had made for you, of course?'

'No, I had no idea.'

'But when we first met in your office you mentioned a family trust.'

Katriona hesitated, seeming not to know how she should reply. Then she said brusquely, 'I made that up.'

'Because you thought I wouldn't take money from you?'

'Yes,' she replied and then, as though she wanted to forget the subject, she continued, 'The question is what do we do now? I can't see how knowing my father's will helps us to decide who killed him.'

An outline of a plan had been forming in Bruce's mind as he had been listening to MacNair's recorded will. He was by no means convinced that it would succeed, but even if it failed no great harm would be done. He began to tell Katriona what he had in mind, working out the details as he was speaking.

'I think we should pretend that we do know who killed your father.'

'For what purpose? To bluff the murderer into giving himself away?'

'Something like that. Whoever it is probably thinks by now that we do know. He or she will be aware that we found something which your father hid in the bothy.'

'What are you suggesting?'

'Have you heard of the domino effect? If a row of dominoes is positioned the right distance apart, each one standing vertically, and you knock the first one over, it will fall against the second and knock that over. The second knocks down the third and so on until the whole row is down.'

'Sounds like one of those theories management consultants invent to prove how clever they are!'

'It is. Now let's see whether we can make it work.'

Picking up the telephone on MacNair's desk, Bruce dialled the number of the *Glasgow Chronicle* and asked to speak to Maggie. It took the switchboard girl a couple of minutes to track Maggie down, but presently she was on the line, curiosity straining at the seams of her voice.

'What's this? A night on the ram? Don't tell me you've breached the lady solicitor's defences.'

Bruce ignored the gibe. 'What would you do if I were 'phoning in a story for your paper?'

'Take it down.'

'Then take this down.'

The story which Bruce dictated to Maggie had no frills. Katriona MacNair, the daughter of Iain MacNair, whose body had been washed up on the shore at Stranraer, would be holding a press conference at six that evening in her late father's house at Bridge of Allan.

At the press conference she would play a tape recording which her father had made shortly before he had been murdered.

'Is that all?' Maggie asked.

'What more do you want? A public execution?'

'I'll need a bit more if we're to send someone out there to cover the press conference.'

'What I read you is the statement. But for your private information the tape will very likely reveal why MacNair was murdered.'

'You can do better than that, Bruce darling. Give me a clue.'

'I can't Maggie, really. But I will say this. Among other things in the tape recording which MacNair left is his will. It mentions a trust which he set up for his daughter of which the trustees are Sir Douglass Tweedie and his partner Peter Wandercliff. But more interesting than that, one of the bequests is to his divorced wife, Mrs Brenda Ferguson.'

'Is she the wife of the bookie?'

'Yes. They live in Drymen.' Bruce gave Maggie the telephone number of the Fergusons.

'You're saying you want me to 'phone her?'

'Isn't that what a good journalist would do?'

'Bruce you shit! You're using me!'

'Yes, and don't send any of your reporters nosing around will you? Not before six anyway.'

Maggie laughed good-naturedly. 'My God, you're devious! But I'll do it for you, pet.'

As he had been speaking to Maggie, Bruce had been watching Katriona's face and he seemed to detect a change in her attitude. The reserve and suspicion which, he had thought, had slowly evaporated during the night they had spent together on Ardnamurchan seemed to return and he sensed that she disapproved or was annoyed by what he was doing.

When he put the 'phone down she remarked, 'If your friend calls my mother she'll be round here faster than a nuclear-powered missile.'

'Good! Then the first domino will have been toppled.'

171

## 19

EVER SINCE THEY had arrived in MacNair's study, Bruce had been bothered by an elusive idea which had been hovering in the recesses of his mind without taking shape. Looking back, he realized that it had first begun to nag at his consciousness when his glance had fallen involuntarily on the filing cabinet. Now, as he recalled his search through the cabinet on his first visit to the house and what he had found inside it, the idea began to take recognizable form. The sheets of paper on which MacNair had written his notes were still in his pocket and he took them out and unfolded them. After smoothing out the creases he turned them over and examined the delivery orders carefully.

Then he opened the middle drawer of the filing cabinet and flicked through the documents and papers inside until he found what he wanted, the letter signed by Dougal Cairns, manager of Glen Cromach distillery, confirming that, in accordance with MacNair's instructions, two hogsheads of whisky had been shipped down by road to the Loch Rannoch Whisky Company.

'When that American consulted your firm about the whisky his father had bought,' he said to Katriona, 'did he have a delivery order like these, do you know?'

'He had some proof of ownership, but I'm not certain precisely what it was.'

'Would your partner have kept it?'

'No, but there would almost certainly be a copy in the file.'

'Could you check on that?'

'Surely. I can ring the office and find out.'

'Then give them a call now. It could be important. And ask whether the numbers of the casks he bought are on the document.'

Leaving her in the study to make the call, Bruce went exploring. He had no idea where a man like MacNair would keep his guns and fishing rods. There did not appear to be a room in the house designed for that purpose, so he decided to try the bedrooms. Of the two larger rooms, MacNair had evidently been using the one nearest to the entrance hall of the house. It had a built-in unit running along the full length of one wall with wardrobe space, shelves and a dressing table. In it he found MacNair's suits, shirts, underwear and shoes all neatly arranged, by Mrs Duncan no doubt. There were two doors in the opposite wall, one of them partly open which led to the bathroom. The other door was locked but he found the key to it in a drawer of the dressing table. Opening the door he saw that it led into a closet, almost large enough to be a small room, but without windows. From the disorder in the closet he guessed that Mrs Duncan had never been allowed inside it. Fishing rods, gaffs, waders were stacked haphazardly against the walls along with an assortment of shooting sticks, two sets of golf clubs, one Wellington boot, a badly warped squash racquet, binoculars, a pair of Purdey shotguns and a Rigby sporting rifle. On a shelf at the back were boxes of cartridges for the shotguns and bullets for the rifle.

Bruce took the rifle, loaded four rounds into its magazine, although he was sure he would never have the chance to use more than one, and drew the bolt back and then pushed it back to feed the top round into the chamber. After putting on the safety catch, he replaced the rifle in the closet, leaving it standing against a wall in a handy position. When he left the bedroom he did not lock the closet door but left it standing slightly ajar. He found Katriona in the study just finishing the call she had made to her office.

'The parcel of whisky sold to Marshall Friend's father,' she told Bruce, 'consisted of five hogsheads of Glen Cromach Malt whisky. The casks were numbered 8501 to 8505 inclusive.'

The delivery orders on the back of which Iain MacNair had written his notes lay on the desk where Bruce had left them. Picking them up he checked the numbers of the casks which the Bonnie Braes Whisky Company had sold to American investors.

'The numbers of the casks which J. S. Gannon of Tampa, Florida, bought are the same, 8501 to 8505 inclusive.'

'Could it be a typing error?'

Bruce held out the remaining two delivery orders. 'These show that a Pete Neidermacher of Minneapolis and a Mrs Patty Kyle of Los Angeles were both sold five hogsheads of whisky and the casks they bought were numbered 8506 to 8510 inclusive, both of them. And in case you might think that was just coincidence, your father had cask number 8506 shipped down to him from Glen Cromach distillery not many months ago.'

'Is that significant?'

'I believe it explains why your father was murdered.'

'And who murdered him?'

'No, but we may well find that out too, shortly.'

The house had been designed in such a way that the living-room and the two larger bedrooms overlooked the garden at the back, while the kitchen, the bathrooms and the study were all in front. Sanderson went to one of the windows in the study, opened it and listened. The residential roads in that part of Bridge of Allan were always quiet in the afternoons and any unusual noise caught one's attention.

'What is it?' Katriona enquired.

'We may learn the answer to your last question sooner than I imagined. That noise sounded like the engine of a powerful sports car.'

'The Porsche?'

'Could be.'

'Can you see any sign of it?'

'No, but I don't suppose our friend would drive up to the front of the house. He'd park some distance away along the road.'

'You were expecting this, weren't you?' Katriona asked accusingly. 'In fact I believe it's part of your plan. And you didn't tell me.'

'I'm sorry,' Bruce replied and grinned. 'But I didn't want to raise your hopes.'

Her irritation evaporated and she smiled back. 'Bruce, you're incorrigible! What do we do now?'

'Just as a precaution in case it is the driver of the Porsche, we'll hide. But first we'll bait the trap.'

He picked up the microcassette recorder, changed the cassette over to the side on which MacNair had recorded his lengthy plans for the

174

launch of his new whisky product, switched the machine on, turning the volume up to its maximum and set it down on the desk again to play. Leaving the door to the study slightly ajar so that the sound of the recorder would be heard from a distance, they went through the living-room and into MacNair's bedroom.

There was enough room for the two of them in the gun closet, but they had to stand close together and Bruce was conscious of Katriona's physical presence. He became aware too, for the first time since they had met, of a physical attraction, and when their hands brushed against each other he found himself wishing that she would take hold of his. The idea, he knew, was juvenile and ridiculous but as they stood there waiting, it grew gradually stronger. He was curious to know whether the simple physical contact of holding her hand in his would bring any sensuous pleasure and equally curious to see how she would respond. Presently the impulse became a compulsion and he took her hand.

'What's this? Cupboard love?' He saw that she was laughing, but not unkindly, and she did not take her hand away.

After what seemed like a long wait, they heard the sound of breaking glass. It was a gentle sound, coming from a distance and Bruce could imagine a man breaking a pane of glass with no more force than was necessary, making a hole no larger then he needed to thrust his hand through and slip the catch of the window. No more sounds followed, showing that whoever was breaking into the house was doing it quietly and with professional skill.

Then suddenly they were startled to hear the bedroom door being opened. The housebreaker took a few paces into the room and then seemed to pause, perhaps to look around. Bruce had left the closet door very slightly open, not far enough for them to be able to see into the room, but far enough for the intruder to notice it and grow curious. He cursed his stupidity in not closing it and reached for the rifle which stood propped up against the wall not far from him, picked it up and slipped off the safety catch.

But presently they heard receding footsteps and the bedroom door was gently closed. Katriona, who had been standing rigid, her face frozen with tension, closed her eyes with relief. 'What do we do now?' she whispered.

175

'You wait here,' Bruce replied.

'No way. I'm going wherever you go.'

'Then keep behind me.'

Leaving the closet, Bruce went to the bedroom door, opened it cautiously and looked out into the entrance hall. The door opposite him which led into the living-room was open and he could hear the distant sound of a man's voice which, he knew, must be MacNair's coming from the tape recorder in the study. Still holding the rifle he crossed the hall as quietly as he could and looked into the living-room.

A man was crossing the room towards the study door. Like Bruce he was moving cautiously, one slow step at a time, and he too was armed. The short, squat hand-gun he was holding was unlike any weapon Bruce had ever seen before but it looked far more lethal than any rifle. The man himself, powerfully built and dressed in the clothes a man might wear out stalking on the hill, looked as deadly as the gun.

When he reached the partly open door to the study, he stopped for a few moments then, gathering himself, pushed the door wide open with one hand and stepped into the doorway. Immediately Bruce, not giving him time to recover from his surprise at finding the study empty, took two quick paces into the living-room and raised the rifle to his shoulder.

'Drop that gun!' he ordered.

The man turned round slowly, his expression showing neither alarm nor astonishment, nothing more than a hint of a smile. Bruce saw the muscles of the hand in which he was holding the gun tighten almost imperceptibly and knew he was going to fire. So he fired first. The rifle bullet struck where he was aiming, just behind the right kneecap. He knew as he squeezed the trigger that he was taking a reckless chance, that he should have had the rifle pointing at eyes or throat or heart.

His shot was not in time to stop the man firing but the impact of the rifle bullet knocked him off balance. His hand-gun seemed to explode with a shattering roar and suddenly there was a huge hole in the wall just below the ceiling and the floor was covered in plaster and debris. Yelling an obscenity the man collapsed, grabbing at his knee and the gun fell from his grip and slid away from him across the floor. Frantically he rolled over and began crawling towards it. Stepping forward swiftly, Bruce swung the butt of the rifle down and held it threateningly above the man's face.

'Stay where you are, friend,' he told the man. 'Don't even move an inch.' Then over his shoulder he called out to Katriona, 'Pick up his gun.'

Stung into a fury by either his helplessness or pain or both, the man began to swear, hissing obscenities through partly clenched teeth. Blood was spurting from the wound behind his knee in a way that suggested the bullet had pierced an artery. Clutching at his leg he writhed on the ground and the obscenities turned into grunts of pain, animal noises reminiscent of an abattoir.

'We must do something,' Katriona said, 'or he'll bleed to death.'

'I don't know why we should be concerned if he did, but you had better call an ambulance.'

She went into the study heading for the telephone, but before she reached it they heard the front door bell ring, followed immediately by a thunderous banging as though someone were beating on it with their fists.

Katriona left the room to see who it was and when she returned she was accompanied by Chief Inspector Forbes and two men who, Bruce assumed, must be policemen in plain clothes. Forbes checked for an instant as he entered the room, taking in the implications of what he saw. Then he strode across to Bruce and reached for the rifle.

'I'll take that,' he said firmly.

With the rifle in his hand he looked down at the wounded man on the floor who stopped cursing and moaning and looked back at him sullenly.

'So,' Forbes said, 'it's you is it, laddie? Our old friend the Clydeside cowboy, Jimmie Bryce.'

## 20

EFFICIENTLY BUT NOISILY, and with a good deal of swearing, Forbes took charge. One policeman was told to put a tourniquet on Bryce's leg and the other sent in search of towels to mop up the worst of the blood. Forbes himself telephoned for an ambulance and, when it appeared, Bryce was taken off to the nearest hospital accompanied by one of the men.

'Now, sir,' Forbes said to Bruce when the ambulance had left. 'Will you tell me how you came to be involved in this private war?'

'If I hadn't shot him, he'd have killed us both.' Bruce pointed at the gaping hole in the wall of the living-room. 'And as you can see, I shot to wound.'

'You were fortunate to shoot first. Jimmie Bryce has never shown any great concern for other folk's lives. But why did he come after you?'

'Someone must have paid him to. I've not seen the man before.'

'That may be, but you've not answered my question. Why would anyone want you and the young woman killed?'

Bruce took MacNair's notes from his pocket and held them up. 'It can only have been because of these.'

He told Forbes how Katriona and he had found the papers in the bothy where her father had hidden them and how Bryce had fired at them and then followed them in the Porsche as they drove south. Forbes's expression as he listened was a nice blend of incredulity and suspicion and when Bruce had finished he reached for the notes.

'Before you read the papers, Inspector, I'd like to ask you a question. Why did you come here this afternoon?'

'We were looking for you.'

'But why did you come to Bridge of Allan?'

'We went to Edinburgh this morning, meaning to ask Miss

MacNair some questions in connection with her father's death. We were told that she had driven up to the Highlands with you yesterday and not returned; that she'd been away all night. So we began looking for the pair of you.'

'Did you think we were on the run?' Bruce taunted him gently.

Forbes ignored the question. 'Then we checked back and saw that Mr MacNair had owned a house in Bridge of Allan. So we came here on the offchance of finding you. Why do you ask?'

'I wondered whether anyone had told you we were here.'

'Who could have told us?'

'Why not read those notes first, Inspector. Then I'll explain.'

Reading MacNair's notes on his brand of immature whisky would tell Forbes nothing he needed to know, but Bruce was playing for time. The plan which he had put in train by 'phoning Maggie needed time to take effect and if Forbes were told too much now he might spoil it. Fortunately Forbes was a slow, laborious reader and he had not even finished the second page of the notes when they heard a car pull up outside the house. It was Katriona's mother and Jock Ferguson in the red Jaguar and Katriona opened the door to them. Their raised voices could be heard coming from the hallway but Katriona made no reply to their questions as she led them into the living-room. Ferguson seemed stunned to find the police there.

'Good God, Forbes! What are you doing here, man?'

'I'm beginning to wonder about that myself. And I might ask you the same question.'

'This is a family matter,' Mrs Ferguson said firmly. She was a small, gold-plated woman, fighting to hold on to middle age with the same self-centred dedication as in middle age she had no doubt fought to hold on to her youth, but without any conspicuously greater success.

'My mother has come to hear my father's will,' Katriona explained to Forbes.

'Hear? What do you mean hear the will?' Brenda Ferguson asked sharply.

'It's not in writing. He recorded it on tape. You can listen to it later if you wish, but I can save you the suspense of waiting. Daddy left you the house in Drymen.'

'Is that all?'

'All?' Katriona said indignantly. 'You had no reason to expect anything.'

'Did you tell anyone else that you and your husband were coming here, Mrs Ferguson?' Bruce asked.

'I told Douglass Tweedie what that reporter woman said about Kate holding a press conference. He has a right to know, if he's going to be accused of misappropriating trust funds.'

'What's this about a press conference?' Forbes had been prepared to wait in the wings, watching the action patiently because he sensed that he would learn more that way than by asking questions, but like most policemen, resentful of the way the media was always ready to attack the police, the mention of a press conference made him uneasy.

'Did Iain leave your mother no cash at all?' Ferguson asked suddenly. The will was more important to him than any press conference.

'Why not play the tape through and hear the will for yourselves?' Bruce suggested.

'Yes, I think we should,' Brenda Ferguson agreed. She had, it seemed, not ruled out the possibility that her daughter had deliberately misled them.

After rewinding the tape in the cassette, Bruce set the recorder to play. As the others were listening to MacNair's words, Katriona came up to Bruce and whispered, 'What are you expecting to happen next?'

'Sir Douglass Tweedie to arrive, I hope.'

'So he's the second of your dominoes?'

'If I'm right, yes.'

In the event Bruce was only partly right. Not many minutes later, while the tape was still playing, Sir Douglass and Peter Wandercliff arrived at the house, but they came together, driven by a chauffeur in Tweedie's Rolls Royce. The remaining policeman who had come from Glasgow with Forbes let them into the house and Sir Douglass strode into the living-room followed by Wandercliff. It was the first time that Bruce had seen Tweedie standing up and he was surprised to find that he was a small man, but like many small men he was able to impose his presence and his authority on other people with a combination of self-confidence, egotism and aggression.

180

'What's all this about, young lady?' he asked Katriona loudly and it was clear that he was not ready to believe whatever answer she might give him.

'Sir Douglass! I was not expecting you,' Katriona said brightly, perhaps a little too brightly.

'I have no doubt as to that, but let's hope I have come in time to prevent you making an expensive mistake.'

'What mistake is that?'

'Slander. If at your press conference you were to make any allegations that we had mishandled your father's trust, Wandercliff here and I would have no choice but to sue you.'

'Your father would never have suggested that we had misappropriated the money!' Wandercliff protested. 'I won't believe it!'

'Have you any idea of the mischief you would be doing?' Tweedie continued. 'Accusations like that, even though they are totally untrue, could throw doubts on my integrity. Think what damage you would do to my reputation and that of my bank!'

'I can't imagine why you should suppose that I was going to impugn your integrity,' Katriona said. 'I've no doubt at all that your handling of the trust has been exemplary.'

'That's not what the reporter hinted to your mother.'

While they were talking, Brenda Ferguson had been listening to MacNair's tape recording. Now the message had reached its end and as Bruce switched off the machine she turned to Tweedie.

'Iain left a will on tape, Douglass. He mentioned that he had set up a trust for Kate but nothing more. He certainly made no accusations against you or Peter.'

'I should hope not indeed!' Tweedie turned to Wandercliff. 'It seems we've been brought out here on false pretences, Peter.'

'And so have we,' Ferguson said sourly.

'None of you was brought here, Sir Douglass,' Bruce said. 'All four of you were only too eager to come, although one of you is disappointed, I've no doubt.'

'Why should we be disappointed?'

'Because one of you will have been hoping to find that Katriona and I were dead. If Bryce had been a shade faster with his gun we would have been.'

181

'Who the hell's Bryce?' Tweedie demanded.

'The man who killed Katriona's father.'

'A professional thug,' Forbes added. 'Apparently he tried to kill these two young people but Mr Sanderson shot him first.'

'Is he dead?'

'No, only wounded. He's away to the hospital in an ambulance.'

Dour though he might be, Sir Douglass Tweedie was also sharp, sharp enough to realize the implications of what Bruce had said before anyone else, including the police. 'You're suggesting that one of us sent this man Bryce here to kill you.'

'One of you must have done. Bryce didn't follow Katriona and me here. We know that. And only the four of you knew we were here.'

'You know Bryce, of course, Jock. He was one of your boys, was he not? On the payroll?'

Katriona's question, clearly not as casual as she made it sound, was too much for Ferguson. He was a slow-witted man, content in the normal way to remain placid and immovable, like an island in a river, while the currents of other people's conversation swirled around him. But now, losing his temper, he began to shout.

'I know what that's supposed to mean. You're hoping to make folk believe I killed your dad.' As he lost control his heavy Glasgow accent became heavier, the vowels broader, the words swallowing each other. 'Why me? Why not you? Tell us that! Who stood to gain most from Iain's death? And you always hated him, spoilt, stuck-up little bitch that you were. It was only when you knew your mother was asking him for a loan that you started making up to him.'

'A loan? That's a nice word for it! She wanted to take him to court.'

'Maybe when you found out how much he was leaving you, you decided to get your hands on it as quickly as you could,' Mrs Ferguson said, joining her husband in attack.

'And you knew Jimmie Bryce. I mind how he used to come to the house sniffing after you when you were just a lass. And did you no fancy him yourself a wee bit?' Maybe the two of you worked out how to kill your dad.'

Brenda Ferguson turned to Bruce. 'How do you know that Bryce came here to kill the pair of you? He may have been after you alone. And are you sure she didn't tell him you were here?'

The unexpectedness of the last question almost threw Bruce off balance. He recalled that Katriona had been alone in the study 'phoning her office while he had been looking for her father's rifle. She had been alone long enough to make another call. He put the thought out of his mind. Any doubts he may have had about Katriona had been demolished by a simple piece of deduction. Logic told him that whoever had arranged for MacNair's death had also been responsible for the earlier attempts on his life. Bryce had been waiting on the road from Drymen to Stirling in the stolen juggernaut and he must have been told what time MacNair's Bentley would be coming along towards him. A 'phone call to a prearranged number would have warned him that MacNair had left for home and the call could only have been made by one of the guests at Mrs Ferguson's dinner party. Bruce might have explained that to the Fergusons but he chose another, more direct route.

'Money was the motive behind the murder of Mr MacNair,' he remarked. 'But not his money.'

'What does that mean?' Forbes asked quickly.

'He was killed not so that someone could inherit a fortune but to protect one.'

'Man, you're talking in riddles!' Tweedie exclaimed.

MacNair's notes were lying on the table where Forbes had left them. Bruce picked them up once more. 'Together with the tape recording of his will, Mr MacNair left three pages of notes on the production, packaging, marketing and advertising of a new product he intended to launch for the Loch Rannoch Whisky Company.' He showed the sheets to the others. 'These explain why he was murdered.'

Sir Douglass Tweedie reached out, snatched the notes from Bruce and began reading them impatiently. One sensed that he was concerned about what Iain MacNair might have written.

'The notes will tell you nothing,' Bruce said. 'But look at the other sides of the sheets on which they are written.'

Tweedie did as he told him. 'They're just delivery orders for whisky. The Bonnie Braes Whisky Corporation? I've never heard of it!'

'You were not meant to hear of it. It was an outfit set up in New

York to sell new whisky to unsuspecting Americans.'

'Whisky investments? Oh, yes a number of companies were set up to do that and it did the reputation of the Scotch whisky industry a great deal of harm.'

'Their business was legitimate, though, even though investors may have been misled. Bonnie Braes was working a different angle and one that was no more than a con game, a complete fraud.'

Tweedie looked at the delivery orders more closely as he might have inspected a dubious balance sheet. 'Are you saying the company sold worthless scraps of paper? That there was no whisky?'

'There was some whisky. A few hogsheads of Glen Cromach Malt. That's true isn't it, Wandercliff?'

Wandercliff appeared confused by the question. 'Why do you ask me?'

'Did you ever do any business with these Bonnie Braes people, Peter?' Tweedie asked.

Wandercliff frowned, as though remembering were an effort. 'I believe I may have done in my broking days. The name is certainly familiar.'

'You did business with them all right,' Bruce told him. 'You set the company up. Just a paper company, I imagine, one guy operating out of an office in New York; a front man with good contacts who may have placed a few discreet advertisements in the financial papers and had a supply of glossy brochures to send out. A simple operation and not expensive.'

'Nobody could make much out of selling a few casks of whisky.' Forbes threw the remark out like a fisherman casting a fly. He had become very interested in what Bruce was saying.

'Don't you believe it! Wandercliff made a million. With the connivance of the distillery manager at Glen Cromach, he sold the whisky over and over again to different investors.'

'That's a monstrous accusation!' Wandercliff protested, but there was little fire in his indignation.

'Have you any proof?' Forbes asked Bruce.

'Here's the proof.' Bruce took MacNair's notes back from Tweedie and held them up. 'Until recently one could have found a good many more delivery orders like these, hidden in the old records

184

of Wandercliff's company. Katriona's father may have thrown some of them away. The rest were no doubt burnt in that very convenient fire last Saturday night.'

'What is the connection between this and the murder of Mr MacNair?' Forbes asked.

'When you returned from your honeymoon cruise,' Bruce told Wandercliff, 'you found that Katriona's father had been going through all the company's old records, with the intention of cutting down the volume of paper and rationalizing the filing system. You saw that some of the old delivery orders made out in the name of Bonnie Braes were missing. He may have also told you that he'd found discrepancies in the cask numbers of the twelve-year-old whisky he had recently ordered from Glen Cromach distillery and that he was going to take the matter up when he visited the distillery. Or perhaps Mrs Hastie told you. No doubt he thought it was a genuine mistake, but you knew that if he checked the distillery records he would find out the truth.'

'Iain would never have condoned it,' Tweedie said. 'Whatever his faults he was honest, sometimes tiresomely so.'

'Precisely. That was why Wandercliff had to have him killed.'

Everyone in the room looked at Wandercliff. Although he still seemed composed and assured, his eyes held a wild fear, like those of a hunted animal. 'I've never heard anything so absurd,' he began and Bruce wondered whether he was going to meet the accusation with brazen denials or some kind of bluff. Then suddenly he leapt across the room, brushing Forbes aside. The sporting rifle had been placed by one of the policemen standing against the wall in a far corner of the room. Taking advantage of surprise, Wandercliff reached it before the remaining policeman, who had been standing by the door, could stop him. Picking up the rifle, he spun round and pointed it in the direction of Bruce and the others around him.

'Put that down, man,' Forbes said calmly. 'It will do you no good.'

'I'm not going to give up everything,' Wandercliff said. 'Everything I've worked all these years for.'

'What are you going to do? Kill us all?'

'If I have to, yes.'

'There are not enough bullets in the magazine to shoot us all,' Bruce said.

185

'Don't try to bluff me!' Wandercliff sneered. 'Do you think I know nothing about rifles? I've been shooting on the wealthiest estates in Scotland.'

They all saw his thumb move as he slipped off the safety catch. Slowly, still pointing the rifle in their direction, he moved towards the door which led from the living-room into the entrance hall. The hand-gun which Bryce had been carrying lay on the dining-table which stood against one wall of the room next to the serving hatch which opened on to the kitchen. Wandercliff glanced at it, wondering perhaps whether it might be a more effective weapon than the rifle.

'Don't be an idiot,' Bruce said and began walking towards him. 'Give me the rifle.'

'Stay where you are. It will be a pleasure to kill you, I can tell you. You and your meddling.'

Ignoring the threat, Bruce continued moving in his direction. Forbes said quickly, 'Don't try anything sir. He'll shoot.'

When Bruce was not more than a few feet from him, Wandercliff seemed to hesitate. Then he raised the rifle to his shoulder and with the muzzle pointed straight at Bruce's heart, pulled the trigger. Brenda Ferguson screamed but the scream came too late to drown the click that came from the mechanism. As Wandercliff looked down at the rifle in bewilderment, Bruce and the policeman rushed him. He fought savagely, shouting curses and, in his fury, relapsing into Dutch, but they knocked him to the floor and as Bruce knelt on him the policeman handcuffed his wrists behind his back.

'That was foolhardy of you, sir, if I may say so,' Forbes said sternly to Bruce as he picked up the rifle and examined it.

'Not really. I knew there was only a spent round in the chamber because after shooting Bryce I didn't draw the bolt back to eject it.'

The drama petered out in anticlimax. More police arrived from the local station and Wandercliff was taken away. Sir Douglass was driven back to Glasgow in his Rolls and presently Brenda and Jock Ferguson left, without ceremony and without a parting word to Katriona, as though their resentment had only been sharpened by learning that she was not responsible for her father's death.

'We'll need statements from you both in due course,' Forbes said as the police were preparing to leave. 'As far as I can see the evidence against Wandercliff doesn't amount to much.'

'Try making a few enquiries in Portugal. You may well be able to prove that Bryce murdered Fraser, the distillery manager from Glen Cromach, as well. Piece it all together and you'll maybe get a confession from Wandercliff.'

'I doubt that. He fought like a wild thing, did he not?'

'Yes. It was as well you had brought those handcuffs with you.'

Forbes looked at Bruce. The expression on his face was as dour as always but the corners of his eyes were wrinkled in what could only have been a smile. 'We had them handy, sir, thinking we might need them to use on you.'

## 21

'How can you tell when it's ready?' Katriona looked into the pan on the cooker. 'Do you time it?'

'Nothing so scientific. I go by the look of it, the colour and the consistency.'

'Whenever I try it ends up either watery or a glutinous, tasteless lump.' She laughed. 'A Scottish girl who can't cook mince and tatties! Weird isn't it?'

'The simple dishes are often the most difficult to cook well.'

They had decided to have supper at her father's house. By the time they had answered the questions of the police and patched up the damage that Bryce's gun had done to the living-room wall, it was early evening, so Bruce had offered to cook a meal from whatever they could find in the refrigerator or the deep freeze.

'How did you learn to cook?' Katriona asked.

'I just picked it up, watching my mother, giving a hand in the kitchen of Neil's hotel and I got plenty of practice living alone in London. In my job I was expected to eat out a good deal and when I was at home I yearned for all the traditional Scottish foods: mince and tatties, stovies, black puddings, porridge, even haggis.'

'Do you cook for that woman you're living with?'

'I don't live with Maggie, I stay with her. Simon was her boy-friend.'

The answer seemed to please Katriona. She asked him, 'Will you teach me to cook?'

'Surely. I'll teach you what little I know, but it will take time.'

'That's all right. I can spare the time if you can.'

While he was still cooking the mince, the telephone in the study rang and Katriona went to answer it. She was away a long time and he had finished the mince and the potatoes, placing them in the oven to keep warm, before she returned. While he was washing the pans she poured them each a whisky from a bottle he had found in the kitchen.

'That was Inspector Forbes calling from Glasgow,' she said. 'He thought we'd like to know that Peter Wandercliff has admitted everything. He's made a full confession but Bryce has said nothing.'

'He wouldn't. Bryce is hard, a real ned.'

'Wandercliff claims that he never meant to defraud anyone.'

'Just to take their money?'

'Not take, use.'

Wandercliff, Forbes had told Katriona, claimed that he had always intended, at the end of twelve years, to buy back the whisky which investors believed they had purchased from the Bonnie Braes Whisky Corporation. He would offer them the current price, which would give them at least a modest profit. He in the meantime would have had the use of their money which he would have invested in ways that would have given him a much larger return. In his view there was nothing immoral in that.

'That may have been his intention when he started,' Bruce commented. 'But he would be expecting that after twelve years a good many of the investors, when they found that Bonnie Braes had gone out of business, would simply lose interest and write their money off. He only did business with wealthy people, I imagine.'

'But if they did try to sell the whisky through a broker the fraud would be discovered.'

'They would have difficulty in selling it. Glen Cromach isn't one of the popular malts. There'd not be much demand for it and certainly not at the price the investors would be expecting. Wandercliff had sold it to them at prices well above the going rate and told them they would make a handsome return on their investment. As a precaution he probably let it be known among the broking fraternity that Loch Rannoch was in the market for twelve-year-old Glen Cromach, so that any enquiries would be channelled back to him. Isn't that what happened with your American client, Marshall Friend?'

'Yes. But why did Wandercliff buy any whisky at all? The deals he was making were just paper transactions.'

'He had to have a few casks, just in case some American investor on a trip to Scotland grew curious and called at the distillery to see his whisky. That does happen, I believe. And if one did Fraser would have shown him the casks he was holding for the Loch Rannoch Whisky Company.'

They sat down facing each other across the dining-table to eat the mince and tatties. During the past few years Bruce had dined with many young women, more often than not in intimate, expensive restaurants in the West End of London, the White Tower, the Boulestin, L'Epicure. One or two had been favoured by an invitation to have dinner in his apartment, but the meals he had cooked them had always been elaborate and accompanied by vintage claret or champagne, dinner parties for some private celebration. None of them that he could recall had given him such pleasure as the simple meal he and Katriona were sharing that evening. It was as though their survival after the danger they had faced needed not a celebration, but the comforting reassurance of a homely supper. He wondered whether Katriona felt the same.

'I remember my mother telling me once,' she said, 'that Peter Wandercliff only came to Scotland with the intention of making a lot of money in a short time and then returning to Holland.'

'That could well be true. He was shrewd enough to see that there was a fast buck to be made from operating on the fringes of the whisky industry by someone without too many scruples.'

'And then he fell in love with Scotland and with a Scottish girl. He saw himself marrying into the aristocracy and ending up as a Scottish gentleman.'

'Yes and so he decided to stay on here and gamble on the chance that his swindle would never be found out. It was a good gamble. There was nothing to connect him with the Bonnie Braes outfit except those copies of delivery orders.'

'Why did he keep them?' Katriona asked.

'He had to so he could check on the transactions Bonnie Braes had made. As Tweedie said, a good many whisky fillings were being sold to American investors at that time. Wandercliff didn't want to buy any Glen Cromach that other brokers had sold. And if any of the old orders had been found, they would have been assumed to be worthless. Your father did that and used them for scrap paper.'

'And there was Fraser, of course.'

190

'Yes. That was why when your father saw there was something odd about the delivery orders, Wandercliff decided to have both him and Fraser murdered to protect himself.'

Katriona seemed to shiver. She was silent for a time and then she said, 'He nearly got away with it.'

'Very nearly. His plan was clever. Fraser's death was accepted as an accident and everyone was ready to assume that your father had been killed in Belfast.'

They had finished the mince and Bruce went to fetch some oatcakes and butter and Caboc cheese which he had found in the refrigerator. Katriona was looking thoughtful as she poured them each another whisky and instinct told him that her mood had changed. She was no longer thinking of the past, of murder and violence and danger, but of the future. She would tell him what she was thinking when she was ready.

Presently she asked him, 'What will happen to the Loch Rannoch Whisky Company? Do you think it can survive?'

'I don't see why not. When he joined Wandercliff your father built up a very efficient production facility at Cumbernauld.'

Bruce told her of his visit to the blending and bottling halls which had not been damaged in any way by the fire. The stocks of whisky which Iain MacNair had laid down as part of his programme to improve the company's blends would also be a considerable asset.

'Why do you ask?' he concluded.

'There is no one to manage the company now. Would you do it if you were offered the job?'

Bruce had always distrusted hypothetical questions. However innocuous they might appear and no matter how innocent the motives of the person who asked them, they could easily become traps, and he had developed an adroitness in parrying them as skilful as any politician's. But this time his intuition told him that Katriona's question went deeper than mere speculation. Cautiously and diffidently she was planning for the future, one step at a time. So he answered her truthfully.

'If I were to manage the company I'd want to make changes.'

'What kind of changes?'

'To move up-market. I'd abandon the private label business and

191

exporting in bulk and go for quality instead.'

'Then you think my father was wrong?'

'To be perfectly honest, I do. Hurt pride and bitterness at the way he'd been treated were clouding his judgement. Quality coupled with its unique flavour have made Scotch the leading spirit in the world. Your father knew that. MacNair's Gold Label has always been a blend of the highest quality and as long as he was with the company your father kept it that way. The answer to the competition of other drinks is not cutting prices and gimmicks and shoddy quality but to rely on the flavour of Scotch, a flavour which none of them can imitate, and to keep it a drink of superb quality.'

'Then what would you do?'

'At Loch Rannoch? The future of Scotch is in top-quality brands: twelve-year-old de luxe blends and single malt whiskies. I would launch a new and very expensive blend, aiming at comparatively small sales but a fantastic profit margin; an exclusive brand with snob appeal.'

As he had been speaking of her father, Bruce had noticed Katriona's face cloud over with unhappiness. Once again her mood had changed. She said slowly, 'What you said about my father is true of me as well, Bruce. Hurt pride and bitterness at being rejected: you could not have described my feelings more accurately.'

He sensed that she did not wish for denials or words of comfort so he said nothing but waited for her to continue. Eventually she said, 'I've been foul to everyone, especially to you. But not any more. Suddenly after the last two days I feel as though I've just come out of a tunnel.'

She might be out of her tunnel but that, Bruce knew, was not an end to the hurt she had suffered. Her bruised emotions would need time to heal; more time than the bruises and scratches which he had noticed on her arms and hands the previous evening. And until the healing was complete, she would need patience and understanding and tenderness. She was sitting with her arms on the table, and reaching out he laid his hand gently on one of hers.

'I almost feel sorry for Wandercliff.'

'Why do you say that?'

He looked into her eyes and smiled. 'The poor fool fell in love with a Scottish girl and his whole life changed. It could happen to anyone.'